ONE DAY

AT TETON MARSH

One Day
at Teton Marsh

SALLY CARRIGHAR

Illustrations by GEORGE *and* PATRITIA MATTSON

UNIVERSITY OF NEBRASKA PRESS
LINCOLN AND LONDON

First Bison Book printing: 1979

Most recent printing indicated by first digit below:
2   3   4   5   6   7   8   9   10

Library of Congress Cataloging in Publication Data

Carrighar, Sally.
   One day at Teton Marsh.

   "A Bison book."
   Reprint of the ed. published by Knopf, New York.
   1. Zoology—Wyoming—Jackson's Hole. 2. Animals, Habits and
behavior of. 3. Animals, Legends and stories of. I. Title.
QL215.C3   1979   591.9'787'5   78–26679
ISBN 0–8032–6302–3

Published by arrangement with Alfred A. Knopf, Inc.

Manufactured in the United States of America

To a boy who matched in himself the bright resilience of the waters that he loved; and sent me to them later, when he was my father.

CONTENTS

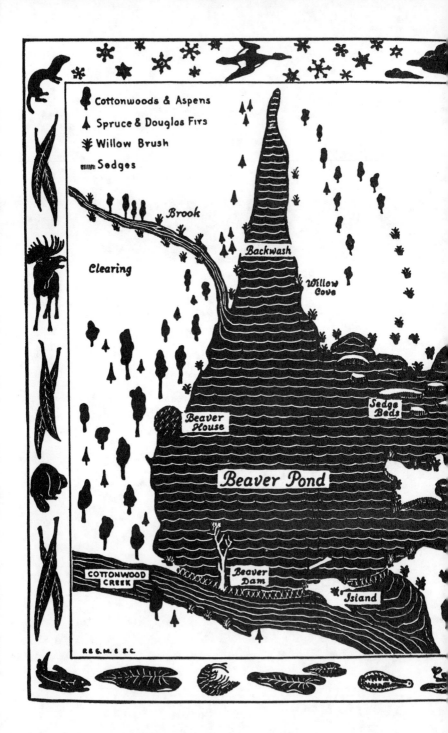

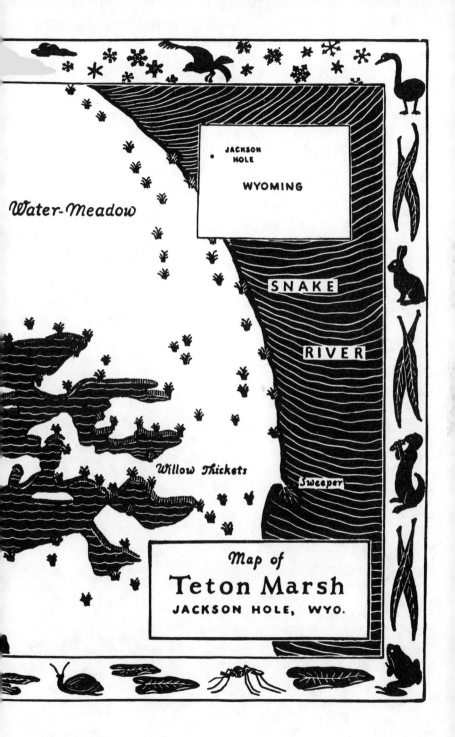

Water-Meadow

JACKSON
HOLE

WYOMING

SNAKE

RIVER

Willow Thickets

Sweeper

Map of
Teton Marsh
JACKSON HOLE, WYO.

The Otter

THE OTTER

☼

And then the peaks along the Teton crest were white, as freshly bright as if the shine of the blue September sky had crystallized upon them. Blown dust had dulled them in the cloudless weather of late summer. Glaciers and snowfields had become a dingy brown, with gleaming stripes where talus rocks slid down them. But as the equinox approached, new snow began to fall. Each morning the frosty sheath on the mountain rim was lower.

Between the snow and timberline the massive barrier had darkened. For the petals had dropped from the asters and alpine sunflowers that had given color to the slope. The lichens had grayed. The juniper and kinnikinnick had drawn their sap back toward their roots.

From down among the crags slow columns of mist were rising, straight until they were caught and combed out by the winds across the saddles. At the bottom of each shaft of vapor was a lake. Since the air was colder than the water now, the lakes would steam until they froze. For a while there would be fragile movement, soft white drifting, upon the shadows of the heavy buttresses.

One phantom pillar toward the north stemmed down to a

little lake on Mt. Moran. At the base of the bare immobile slope it flashed a blue as sharp as the gentians' blue around the shores. The pond was more than water; because of it a fluent company had gathered here. Aspens, firs, and lodgepole pines had framed the granite basin. The banks were mazy with berry thickets. In the shallows wavelets meshed through cat-tails. The animals on the heights — the mountain sheep, black marmots, and grizzly bears — were few and scattered, but every cranny at the lake was sheltering a creature quick to leap, or fly, or swim.

Meltwater from a glacier kept the pond filled. Nearing the shore, it turned in the yellow shade of aspen brush. But that is not the current's core, that brown strand running ahead of the braiding liquid fibres. The flow within the flow is the Otter, hastening home.

He swings through his spine, a vertical wave that tapers down his tail and seems a smoother drive than that of feet, or wings, or wheels. The water resists but with a sinuous, yield-ing pressure. It slips on his short flush fur as it would on oil. He holds his legs close, swaying with his body, till impatience kicks a web-foot out, or one comes down to push him past a snag. A new breath does not slow him. His head arcs through the surface and is lowered by his rolling back. The water's glazed white chill parts on his nose, sheets past his eyes.

With a flickering speed the eyes are altering their inner shape, to sight in the air now, now in the stream, in the tor-rent's fray among the rocks, in foam.

The gaps in the bordering leaves at last were filled with the gloss of the lake instead of the bright air out above the valley. The current cut the bank and fanned off through the pond. A log hung over the water near the inlet. The Otter climbed it.

On the end he lifted to a stand, and a forepaw stroked the air to balance the searching of his nose. That small wide point was darting forward and sideward as he probed the scents.

He was finding many that should have meaning for him; from the pond the smell of fish, his favorite food. He drew it through his nose, not yearning now for the fish but groping for a different odor in it. From the shore he caught the fresh damp mustiness of earth and roots. That was the smell of safety, of nooks deep-shaded by bracken, meadowsweet, and mint. But on this afternoon he needed more than a cover to make him feel secure. He sniffed the longest with his nose turned up to the dusty honey of dry grass blowing with the redolence of pines. The blend was tied in his memory with his family's sunning place.

He peered across the water, which was smooth but wind-pressed, netted with a fine dark veining. No furred head broke its width. The shores had brightened in the two weeks since he and his family went away. The shimmer of the aspens had become more dazzling. That he could see, but not that they were yellow. The daytime world appeared to him as if in brilliant moonlight, without color, for his eyes were formed to find faint gleams, fish in deep pools that an otter must see if nothing else. He discovered the sheen on a raven's breast, which slid along the feathers as the bird turned; and the white feet drawing farther under a varying hare; and the sway of the pine trunks, pinching the streaks of sky. But where was the shadowy movement that he sought?

He dropped on all paws, face to the pond. Clinging with hind feet widely spread, he bent his head below the log. He had not outgrown as yet his dread of diving, but eagerness now curled him over in a fall.

Rapidly he was across the lake, had reached the tunnel in the cat-tails where his mother had taught him to come ashore. Passing the rock where his family ate their fish, he ran along a path beneath the plumes of bluejoint grass. He was going to the knoll where the otters had gathered for their play.

His chin and the tip of his tail were tilted up, and he called in a chirping whistle. That was a challenge to his twin to meet him at the end of the path. Soon the two would pile together in a whirl, a weaving spin, an exercise in speed. The game would train them to catch their food. They need not practice anger, since there was no combat in an otter's capture of a fish, but they must practice swiftness. They also were discovering joy; their nips and slaps, their cries, were bright as splashes. Perhaps a creature's muscles only reach their lightest pace if light hearts have released them. The Otter could overtake a fish with a buoyant ease that surely must exist first in his nerves.

Open sunshine showed ahead. He rushed — but melted to a stop. No otter family rolled on the flattened grass. An elk was there, front knees now tipping his huge bulk to his feet. The small one shrank away and fled to the shore and even the rocks and pondweeds at the bottom of the lake.

The place he should seek his family, at least his twin and mother, was the hollow fir tree on the east bank. There he was born, there he had slept when the family's later wanderings brought them back to the lake. The upper entrance to the tree was through the bark, behind a mountain ash. At that opening his father had left the fish he caught for the kits. But the entrance the others used was underwater, leading from the bank up through the roots.

The young one went in now and, climbing through the moist earth reached the dim clean space within the tree. He turned around, his nose on the woody fibres clawed down by his mother for their bed. Still strong was the scent of the other two. Combined with the odor of his mother's milk, that scent of fur and otter musk had been his whole world in the first five weeks before his eyes were open. He sucked it into his nostrils on this afternoon.

But suddenly he darted from the upper exit. He raced away to a fallen pine tree that he knew and, creeping under, lay and trembled. When his shaking quieted, he shrank into the deeper hideaway of sleep.

What had happened in his mind? Although it might not join two facts to give him understanding, it was brilliantly alert to intuition.

No doubt he could remember a startling thing that had happened recently, back up the glacial stream. His father had gone his own way in the last few weeks, but the other three had stayed together. On that morning they were sleeping in a patch of meadowsweet above the brook. Awakening, eager to play, he had tumbled on his brother. With a growl like a maddened little moan the twin had drawn away; he was engrossed in the autumn sunlight, something to reach for, not quite satisfying. The Otter's mother, pushed with a coaxing nose, had given him only a slit glance. He had left them then, to weave down toward the stream.

He had lain on a sand bar till he saw the blue sway of a chub and sped through the current in a chase that ended with a clean bite. That was the instant when the very mountain jarred.

A towering rock, pried off by water freezing in its cracks, had split from the slope. It struck above the bank and started an avalanche of shale. While crashes thundered over him, the Otter froze in terror. But finally the sliding earth, the boulders, and upturned trees found resting places. Again the only sounds were the water's breaking and the fine high hiss of foam.

He had climbed the bank but found no trace of his mother and twin. For two days he had searched, on the third day left, alone, to return to the lake. The nearer he came to the scenes associated with his family, the brighter was his mood. In his memory of his home, the others were always there. When he did not find them, he did not need to know why they were gone. It was enough that, while he was in the hollow tree, his urge to hunt them suddenly drained away.

When he awoke, he lifted his nose and tried the scents mechanically. Then he dropped his chin across his tail and looked out over the lake. Daylight was almost gone, with no shine now on the tops of the trees nor even the edges of the peaks. The wind had entered its twilight lull; the water was smooth except for the insects' hairline rings, all widening at the same unhurried pace. Around the shores the lake was deeply black. In the center it was a flat reflection of the pale white sky.

The darkness of the lower thicket ruffled with a quiet stir of wings. One twig dipped sharply; the bird was gone. A late kingfisher, curiously silent, skimmed across the lake; at the other side was lost in the gloom among the pines.

The Otter uncoiled with a smooth speed, left the log, and walked down into the water. Up and down his tail swung, pushing him along in shallow scallops with no sound. He was not looking for fish, not searching at all, and yet he sped across the pond. He could relax, but the first of his motions showed his gently urgent nature, as if some hungering, not for prey nor any definite thing, intensified each mood.

He paralleled the east shore, just beyond the jagged border

of the trees' reflection. Nearing the outlet of the lake, he left the water, and the rippling trees shrank back. Not wishing to fish, what should he do? He could polish his fur. A slick coat aided an otter's swimming. He pushed his neck along the sand and scraped ahead on his belly and sides with a doubling and straightening so limber that it seemed he had no spine, no stiffening except the firmness of his muscles. He shook the sand from his fur. What now? He stood and thrust his nose among the odors.

He came to a sharp stop. Down on all feet he began a whip-like swing along the ground. Faster he glided away beneath the brush. He had found his father's scent and by the minute strengthening of it, print to print, went forward on it.

The trail was easy to follow, for his father's short legs gave him a close-set track. The young one moved with the same low swaying gait, a swimmer's, no abrupt steps, more a pressure on the ground learned by his push against the water. The gait would carry him from stream to stream but not as rapidly on land as, for example, the lightly tapping stride of a similar-sized fox.

The tracks descended the mountain through an open stand of pines, new country for the little Otter, dark, with everything strange except the good strong odor under his nose. That muskiness was companionable, almost as if he were hearing his father's call or seeing glimpses of his tail, quick-drawn behind the rocks.

Smell, here, how his father had played along this log, up on the top and weaving among the snags, high spirits expressing themselves in lovely motion. Approaching a creek, the odor band was wide, a slide into the water. The footprints up the bank showed that his father had climbed and ridden down innumerable times. The young one found where he had left the stream on the other side. Below the slope he reached a pool of odor in a stump where his father probably had slept; beyond that, streaks in the grass where he had slid. What lively games a kit could have with this father, who had kept his playfulness as he grew older, who always would be young. In his son this night was no play, only an eagerness to reach the vanishing feet.

He began to smell a mist, a fishy dampness meaning that water was ahead. The odor must have drawn his father too. From here the tracks led straight, through a cover of choke-cherry brush and then out onto sand. Beyond was Leigh Lake, larger than the Otter's pond. He followed his father's trail to the edge of the waves. It ended there. His father had entered the water, which held no tracks, protecting an animal but erasing, too, the odor of one sought with affection.

If the older otter had known that his kit was alone, he would have assumed the later training usually left to a mother. The young one, born the previous spring, could catch his own food and defend himself, but soon the only world he knew would be withdrawn beneath a deep white stillness. The high-stream fish would have gone down into the lakes, where ice would barricade them. Through the center of the valley flowed the swift Snake River, too turbulent to freeze; some fish would winter there and others in pools around the springs. An experienced otter would know where and would teach a kit. Instinct, however, is a good step-mother and probably could guide this orphan. His greatest danger might be loneliness. Normally he would have had a family to return his sociability until the following spring. If there were no joy in his days, could he solve for himself the problems of this first hard winter? His very sensitiveness had its needs. If his emotional hungers went unsatisfied, his appetite for fish might fail; then weakness steal away his impulse to be out and living. And the cold, as deadly as any fang in Jackson Hole, would lie at the entrance of any shelter he might find.

As he had approached Leigh Lake, the forest had become a tree-high tangle, grass rising into boughs of dogwood and mountain ash, those lifting among spruces, and the spires of the spruces into the tufts of lodgepole pines. The trees sheered down abruptly at the lake.

Behind the Otter now a rising wind searched through the leaves. Ahead was only a dark wide prowling, water but with no invitation in it. The strip of sand where he stood was lighter, and strewn with bone-white beaver cuttings. Pale too in the night was the splash of the waves, which were slapping the sand, to pull away and slap it again, to rush up the shore and make another pounce.

The Otter ran along a drift of needle fragments and collapsing foam. He hesitated, ran a little farther, rose on his hind feet, nervously sniffed the wind. He walked a short way into the water, stopped with his head up and his eyes intensely peering. But the end of his tail was limp. The water was catching it about as if it were a strand of pondweed.

Should he return to his own lake, lonely but familiar? Some coming event was known there. The grasses were too brightly polished, and crystals were needling out from the shoreline in the coves. But the grasses did stand, and the flash of fish still crossed the ripples' flash; should he go back? Instinct now gave him the first proof of her care. His tail tensed, he walked forward; then was swimming out to meet the waves.

He pushed along with his porpoiselike roll. But all the lake was thrusting against him, to move backward with a drag. Or did it only seem so, because he had not eaten in the three days since the stream-side tragedy? He soon tired. Turning lower in the lake, he swam with a shallower sculling, easier and faster here where he could grip the water both below him and above.

He was in the first of a chain of lakes that lay like giant puddles drained from the Teton slope. To such a rapid traveler they were not large. As the night progressed, he passed through three of them.

He came out twice, first on the northern corner of Leigh Canyon. Rising for a breath, he heard the cupping of water among stones. He swam to the point. It was a glacier's ancient dump of boulders, now giving holds to trees among the rocks, and huckleberry brush and bracken with the tiny discs of pearly everlastings white beneath. This was the season when his mother soon would have searched for a shelter, a base for the family's winter rambles, and the same urge made the kit feel pleasure at the sight of the starlit boulders and their crannies, opening dark. He sniffed among them; if he found no owner's scent, stole in and turned his size within the nook. Back at the entrance he would test the air for signs of neighbors. He found the odors of black bear, mink, and an animal he did not know. The new scent lay on this flat rock where a little pile of grass and twigs was spread to dry. The Otter stepped on the rock. It tilted, and a cony's protest piped from beneath. That small hare was a harmless creature, but her voice so startled the Otter that he sprang aside, raced back to the shore, and swiftly swam away. The shocks of his recent days made everything unexpected seem a menace.

Beyond Leigh Lake the range of mountains leaned more

steeply above the west shore. It stretched ahead, a long high hover, shading the water from the light of nearly half the stars. The Otter journeyed south beneath it, now in String Lake, river-shaped, close in against the wall.

He was paddling slowly on the surface, circling from side to side with chin up, every move a question. A fish leapt. In the Otter's nerves, however, the circuit was broken between a flash seen by his eyes and the drive in his tail. He was seeking for something else, perhaps for a wedge that could be his father's head, perhaps more vaguely for anything that would give him comfort. He pushed through water-lily pads to the wooded east shore. There he climbed out onto a log that lay half in the water, half in grass. He curled himself beneath a crotch, enclosed by the feel and smell of wood, and his face began to lose the sharpness of its yearning. He blinked a few times, suddenly was asleep.

The storm that would bring the equinox was swinging down from Canada. This night it was over Idaho, its center whirling toward the Teton wall. The winds that raced ahead of it had swept on east; approaching were the faster currents that circled the storm itself. As they looped around it, they funneled up the oval basin of Jackson Hole.

The storm would affect the life of half a continent. Now it was scratching into the Otter's oblivion with the tiny sleet of dead leaves blown against a stump. A snag creaked, and a piece of driftwood thumped the end of his log. Across his nose a grass blade traced its touch. He twitched his head but could not be rid of it. His ears began to gather the wind's cruel chorus of lifeless things in motion, a sound that seemed the stir of breathing creatures, but was not truly breathing; it was not real. The scraping of a cricket's brittle skin, caught on the log, was like a last dry echo of the insect's summer *query, query, query.*

The Otter found the outlet of String Lake, traversed another lake and came to the outlet of it. The deep drift in the lakes was slight. No senses could perceive it. He swam, however, with so little wilfulness that the flow could give his movements a direction.

The guidance of instinct is like that flow, is like a trail in the water that can be followed although it cannot consciously be scented, seen, or felt. The Otter let it lead him at the end of the third lake. There the waters emptied into Cottonwood Creek, which turned east toward the center of the valley. Joining them was the steep cascade of Glacier Creek. Should he go out or up? The high stream was the kind of water that he knew, bright-shattering and cool-gathering, misting on the dark wet-shine of rocks. And what along Cottonwood Creek, so flatly pouring over a bed of cobblestones?

He took the unaccustomed way. The moon was up and silvering the creek. But soon the shade of stream-side cottonwood trees fell over the bright flow. Feeling safer then, he rode on the surface, under lofty boughs that brushed across the stars and gave them extra sparkle. He let himself be carried by the current, with his hind feet spread to the sides like little floats.

Ahead he began to hear the roaring beat of the Snake, a deep-felt rumble. But he was not to reach the river on this night. For he stopped where the trees drew back to open a wider sky on the north side of the creek. There, instead of a ledge of roots, the stream bank was a wall of rubble, weighted with stones — a beaver dam. The Otter left the creek and grasped his way to the top.

Behind the dam he found a pond, a dusky brimming lustre in the night. A cottonwood grove had spread its branches over the west shore. Curving out from the grove to meet the other end of the dam was a marshy meadow, willow and sedge beds among which gradually the pond was lost. The willows were only light blurs now, for the moon was frosting their up-turned leaves. But the Otter could see that they mingled with the water in a labyrinth of bays and channels, winding lagoons and pools with slim boughs festooned over.

Around the pond on all sides spread the floor of the valley, a sagebrush flat. It reached for the breath as deserts do. Beyond were circling mountain ranges, vastly high — heroic country! But the pond itself was intimately sheltered, the width of the valley not seen here, the lower slopes concealed by the shoreline trees, and the white peaks seeming to be moun-tains in the sky. The pond was enclosed but not confining, with ease for the heart in the very shape of the shores.

The Otter discovered a Beaver, crouched on the wooded bank. His forepaws held a willow branch to his mouth; his chisel-teeth shone motionless upon it. They watched each other with curiosity, not friendliness but respect. With a shat-tering flat smack on the water then, the Beaver dived.

The Beaver and his family had made the pond for them-selves. Around it however, and in it, many other animals were finding the right-sized crannies. From a nook in the dam a shrew ran down to the water, leaving a sharp little wire of scent. A silver-haired bat was skimming a drink. A wake boiled out from the willows, moonlight gleamed on the wet keel of a tail, and a muskrat climbed out on a floating log.

The Otter swam a short way into the pond. He found the Beaver's house, against the bank; beyond it the inlet of a brook. The water from the brook was almost warm. Spring-fed, it would keep the pond from freezing in the coldest winter.

He would come tomorrow again. Tired now, he climbed back down the dam and went to sleep in a jam of driftwood under the south bank.

Morning was in full swing when the kit awoke. He lay on a weathered snag and watched a dragonfly that foraged up and down the creek on shimmering taut wings. The current was passing swiftly. He ignored it. He could ride it to the river, to other new, distracting scenes, but his father would not be there. As the Otter suddenly had lost the urge to seek his mother and twin, so now his mind had given up the sense that he was traveling toward his father. No vague consoling promise made him restless any longer.

He closed his eyes, and his weight sank flatly on the smooth gray wood. For lack of food was thinning out his strength. In a simpler, less intelligent animal no emotional shock could interrupt the drive to hunt. But the Otter was a complex creature. He was lost, alone at only half the age he should have been to face the world without a family. Something would have to give him back a feeling of security, some trace of joy would have to stir in him, before he would wish again to chase his lively prey.

Now the liquid chatter of the creek was topped by a burst of voices, birds' perhaps; he did not know them. He opened his eyes. Inherited impressions gave some meaning to those sounds. The voices faded, and he closed his eyes. But once more came the brightly defiant calls, a gust of vocal playfulness, originating where? In the marsh at the top of the dam, across the creek? Half-automatically the Otter slipped from his snag and swam to the base of the dam. The dam was braced by the root-mound of a dead tree and by a miniature island. He climbed to the island.

Lying below the heads of reed-grass, cautiously he peered from between the blades and for the first time in his life saw ducks. Straight up there tilted a tail, and briefly the bird was headless. It dropped back level, flipped its bill to scatter the moisture and flipped its tail, although the tail was not wet. Several mallards left the pond for a play flight, wings in a huddle that became a spin and then unwound. The linings of the wings fanned white reflections on the ripples. Two gadwalls rubbed each other's cheeks, and opposite cheeks – a game? They drew away and toed the water, squawking challenges. The mallards skated back on the surface, gliding to a stop between wide arcs of rainbowed spray.

The energy of the ducks, their crisp and vivid movements, caught for an instant in the Otter's nerves. A shove with his feet had sent him into the pond, and a scooping dive propelled him to a log that floated near the island. He climbed up on it, over the end with the knack that he had for all things in the water. On top he stretched at full length, holding his head high as he darted glances over the flock of birds that had such fun together. Their games had been the sociable kind that little otters liked.

The ducks were quiet now. Wary and still, they rode the surface, tensely faced in his direction. The sparkles tumbled on the ripples, and aspens shook their delicate glitter out across the marsh. But the ducks were motionless, and the Otter's small, brief curiosity fell away.

He dropped his chin to the log. The wavelets rocked him, and the sunny wind flicked through his fur. Back on his mountains pine trees soaked the sunshine into their darkness. Here the sagebrush floored the valley with a downy sheen. The water itself was twinkling as if all the stars had fallen on it and were tossing there. A bull moose ploughed across the shallows and the sunlight drained from his legs in sheets. A yellow warbler was a knot of it that looped above the grass-grown top of the dam. But the cheerful, unfamiliar brightness made the Otter feel more lonely.

Along the backwash of the pond, beyond the brook, a harrier, a marsh hawk, swayed above the shore. The hawk was searching the lily pads for some late-season frog. Prey that he would have found more tempting, a Varying Hare, was in the water-meadow. She was loping through the grass, so softly bouncing that the gleam of her white fur seemed to melt off into light.

The hawk and the Hare were not aware of each other. The hawk slowed, hovering on the wind, for he had seen a garter snake that warmed itself across a willow bough. With motion swift and sinuous as the snake's, the bird dropped. But the snake had slipped in the pond, escaping him. As the hawk veered up, he came in the Hare's view, and she flung her legs in stronger leaps. They caught the eyes of the hawk, and he swerved her way. The Otter could see both creatures, and he watched how their courses swung inevitably together.

The fever of hunting is contagious to all animals who live on flesh. The Otter's hunger had not wakened, yet he lowered his eyes and sought in the gloom below the waves for a fish. Intuitively he glanced through a stand of pondweeds, through the wiry spokes of milfoil, and a float of pennywort leaves.

Off the shore of the island there, a smooth slip — Trout! The Otter sprang. He and the Trout were a streak across the pond. The Trout dodged off to the side and into the roots of the dead tree, pier in the dam. It slid to a nook in the maze and out of reach. But the Otter will have it. He can see it, in its cavern, holding even its gillbeat; and its staring eye shows terror. The Otter pushed his nose between the roots. But here they were too dense. He searched for a broader gap. His forepaws clutched the fibres, pulled . . . why? Why was he tearing in, attempting to get this fish? He did not want it. His interest suddenly went limp.

He left the dam. The ducks were edging away to the willow thickets. And a raven, watching him from a tree on shore, cried harshly that an enemy had come to the marsh. But if the feel of this place was strange, water, at least, was not. He would comfort himself with its good and soothing touch. He sculled for some time through the surface, back and forth across the pond, supported by the water, with its liquid coolness sliding past the skin of his nose. When he stopped, he rested in the shallows near the island.

While he was floating there, a new bird streamed in over the meadow from the river. Her flight was level and low as she passed the sedge beds. In a quick, abrupt curve, then, she had dived in the pond.

Was she a duck? Yes, a Merganser; more intense than most ducks, though, with a more barbaric spirit. The Otter could see her slice through the depths with feathers tight as scales and swimming faster than many trout. She had risen and, as she peered about her, flung the crest that streamed behind her head. Her eyes had an unapproachable look, as if she wanted, as if she even would seek for, loneliness.

Now she must play in the water, delighting in its flow, a silkier wind, a wind with a shine and, for her, a color. She sprang straight up, was above the pond for a length, cut down in a dive clean, smooth, and sharp as light — and was gone.

The kit, too, loved this water! He swung below the surface, somersaulting, surprising himself. As he rolled to the top, he saw that small round shadows, rimmed with light, were bounding on the side of the drifting log. Reflections of the bubbles broken from his fur, they swung as the water did. He slowly stirred, an eddy swirled away from him, and the figures on the wood, the shadows-in-reverse, were large and melting. A flip to see them better, and the wood was covered with bright flakes that gleamed like trout scales. A trout there on the slick grain, quivering, waiting to be snatched! The Otter flashed ahead, in front of the log turned under and emerged on the farther side. He knew no trout was there, but something in him, caught by the lift and leap of the lights, had wished to tumble. He loafed along the surface with his forepaws on his chest — motionless, but now and then a hind foot suddenly kicked out, as if, inside, a little puff of satisfaction burst.

A point in the meadow formed the open end of the backwash. The tip was a tangle of willow brush. The Otter swam to it, climbed ashore through the roots, and found, within, a bed of marsh bluebells and gentians, screened by the willows. He lay in the flowers, hidden but looking out on the pond.

In from the west a gleam of white came drifting. It widened smoothly — the breast of a Trumpeter Swan. He crossed the ripples with no sway, as evenly and quietly as sunlight pushes back the shade. But the searching of his eyes showed his awareness.

Three cygnets followed, and after them their mother. The father paused to preen a snowy flank, to arch a great white wing and run his black bill through the glistening shafts beneath. The mother drew the young ones to her, and they waited. The father's limber long neck coiled from the fluff, swung forward and upright as the wing was lowered and folded. Together the swans moved toward the sedges. Their whitely metallic sheen, more luminous than dogwood or trillium blossoms, disappeared. And the day was darker, lacking now some edge of unearthly radiance.

In the grove, like one of its blowing shadows, rose and fell the voice of a mourning dove. It was the very voice to speak of loneliness, muted and borne.

Soon the activity at the marsh increased until it overwhelmed the homeless visitor. Now he did not want to join it but to leave it.

The Osprey flew from the tree that braced the dam. He poised and suddenly, unlike any hawk the Otter had seen, plunged for the pond. His dive splashed up a swiftly unfolding water flower, and the Otter recoiled within the willows.

The Bull Moose and two cows thrashed over the backwash in a game or combat, wilder than the summer doings of the moose he had known. Ducks beat through the air. Even the little black-capped chickadee, there, standing on a floating reed, was snatching its sips with a nervous haste, as if the drops were gnats. The animals' motions all were high-strung, for the storm was near now, and its approach disturbed them.

The wind was lashing the pond. So the Otter returned to his nook beneath the driftwood in the creek. From here he could see no restlessness except the tongues of the current, lapping by. He was falling asleep when he heard the almost-animate scream of splitting wood and then a roar. The wind's most violent blow had struck the dead tree, pier in the dam, and had thrown it over. It fell in the pond. The roots were torn from the rubble, and water poured through the break, down into the creek.

The new flow swirled in the Otter's refuge, submerging the snag on which he waited, fearful. He left the drift and climbed the bank behind it. Above the pond a thousand wings flashed in the sun, an airy riot. The Beaver came to examine the gap in the dam, and the Otter drew back under cover.

But curiosity soon sent him across the creek to the pond. He found a harvest of his favorite food that nature could not often furnish. The shores were shrinking; the world of countless little animals was draining out. And what could they do except to mesh about in panic?

The water was striped with fish. Some circled near the dam, some sought the brook, and others were trapped in shoreline pools. Once the Otter paused to watch a stranded scud, and once a salamander, briefly, and went on. He stopped at a puddle where mountain suckers swung in a futile search for an escape. His small relative, the Mink, leapt into the puddle, snatched a sucker, ran with it to the willows, hid it, and returned for more. The Otter's head swayed, following the suckers' motion, but he did not reach for a single fish.

He prowled on the bottom. From every side of the pond the currents were funneling into an irresistible heavy tow that poured through the break. It caught him, took him into its driving core, and hurled him out. Beyond the dam the flow dispersed. The Otter found himself in the creek.

The tumultuous ride had shocked his senses numb, his mind to an instant of delirium. Almost at once he left the creek, climbed over the dam, and dived in the pond again. This time he sought the plunging tide deliberately. Once more it swept him out. The ride was fast, and speed is stimulating to an otter, but it gave him no chance for a flash of grace that would originate in his nerves.

He coasted many times through the gap. Once then, when he entered the pond, he swam to the shallows and there boiled into somersaults. The water held him, let him play in its glossy support, his energy freed for fun. Dry-land animals knew no such buoyancy, birds weren't as light, and fish cleaved the flow but could not curl within its curling. In the lilt and swing of water he had found that he could frolic with no challenge from another creature.

He would have learned that skill more slowly if his mother and twin had lived. By spring he would have had the habit of joyfulness. But in only one day he had taught himself this solitary play, the talent of adult otters and peculiarly sweet.

It would let him live. Now he glimpsed a trout — and swung so swiftly to pursue it that his nose slid back along his tail. He let the trout select the way. It whirled beneath him, raced to the upset tree. As one they wove among the boughs, looped, darted, streaked away. When the trout grew tired, the Otter closed his teeth on the back of its head, pressed, let it go. The bite was intended to goad the fish but only stunned it. Dazed, it sank. The game had ended.

The Otter took the trout in his mouth and, climbing on the fallen tree, lay with it in his forepaws while he tore off bites.

He threw back his head to chop the bones, and closed his eyes as he chewed, but opened them for each new mouthful. What does he see? He is motion caught and held.

Toward the bottom of the pond, steep, partly drained now, slid another otter. It was his father! The young one jumped from the tree. The two were spinning in the water, a greeting, though they only seemed to wrestle with each other. They left the pond and raced along the shore.

Soon snow began to fall. It melted on the silt but possibly reminded the older otter how he crossed the white ground during winter, faster than in summer, with a short run and a forward skate. For now he circled the muddy borders of the pond in the same way, not sliding on the silt as far as he could on deep snow, but exhilarated to be trying.

The snow was a warning to the young one. Suddenly he was obsessed with an urge to find a shelter. If this pond were to be his winter base, he must have a refuge from the bitterest weather. The pond should fill again; even now the Beaver was watching the otters from his house, impatient to begin his mending of the dam. While the father continued skating, the kit was searching along the banks for the opening to some abandoned burrow.

His father called him, for he wanted to start on his wanderings. He would take this kit of his, who seemed to be deserted. The small one came to the dam. His father swung over the top and down the outside toward the creek, along which he was traveling. He barked again, the sharp little tone in which a parent urged its young to follow.

Up on the dam the kit stopped, turned, and sniffed the odors of the pond. He had an almost irresistible longing for a shelter here. And yet affection drew him toward his father. In the hard experience of the last few days he had developed a feeling of responsibility for himself. He could not now go back and be dependent.

A spiral of snow whirled close around him, blinding and soft. As it cleared, he saw what seemed to be an opening beneath a willow. He hurried toward it. Coming nearer, he found that his burrow was only a shaded mat of roots. He began to explore the marsh, the endless waterways among the thickets. But first he tried that skating game on the wet silt.

The Cutthroat Trout

✵

Only a sharpened, seeing look in the Trout's eyes proved that he had wakened. No shift of the eyes had flashed their crystalline shine. The wrongness of some sound had roused him. He peered from his nook along the west shore of the pond; was there a glisten of wet fur in the polished darkness? Or did he see the pale clouds hung in the water, moonlight, which had turned to luminous froth the bubbles clinging to the underwater plants?

His shelter was a groove among the sticks of the beaver house. He was holding himself as still as the sticks, so quiet in their tangle that a slippery ooze had grown upon them. His breathing lightened until the water drained through his gills with no perceptible beat, no pulse to send its circular waves out through the pond, revealing that he lay at the center of them.

From the edge of the Beaver's sunken pile of aspen boughs a string of small globes, faintly silver, smoked to the top. Some animal must have touched a branch and rubbed out air that was held within its fur. The water swayed; the creature had begun to swim. Its stroke was not familiar to the Trout, not one of the rhythms that he knew as harmless or a threat. It had more pulse than the Beaver's paddling or the striding of a moose. It was rougher than the swimming of a fish and heavier than a muskrat's sculling. At first the Trout must steady himself with his fins to keep from being slapped against the sticks. But the underwater waves diminished. The last of them struck the shores and clattered back, a liquid echo. The only motion in the pond then was its regular mottling flow, a current from the brook to the beaver dam.

The surging had torn the film of sleep from a thousand little minds. After it ceased, constrained breaths made the pond seem lifeless. But hunger was a danger too. It rose above the fear of the animals, one by one — of the smallest first. Soon the twinkling prowls of the mayfly nymphs, the quick strokes of the water-boatmen, and the foraging of even tinier creatures mingled in a hum like that of insects in the air, but louder. The lightest sounds were wave-beats in the pond. To the Trout's ears came the twanging of minute activity.

Night was nearly over. The Trout knew by the brightening of the water, by his hunger, and the stiffness in his muscles. He saw the webs of the pelican start to push the bird's breast over the top of the pond. Its wing-tips dipped in the water, the webs were shoveling back with greater vigor, the breast was shrinking upward. Only the kick of the feet now broke the surface. When the bird was gone, the fin on the Trout's back stood a little higher, and a ripple scalloped from its front edge to the rear.

The Beaver swam to the entrance of the house and climbed in onto the floor. His angry voice came through the wall. He was driving from his bed the muskrat he allowed to share his home. The feet of a mother moose and her calf had waded off the bank. They dragged their splashes down the shore to a patch of horsetail. The big soft muffles plunged beneath the surface, closed around the plants and pulled them dripping from the water. Even yet the Trout would not risk showing himself. He was the wariest of all the animals in the pond.

Beside the stranger's threat, a more familiar danger kept him hiding. Three times a day the Osprey dived in the pond for fish. The Trout's good time-sense held him under cover when its strike was due: at dawn, as soon as the hawk could see its prey; at noon; and at sunset, with the first receding wave of light. Most mornings the Trout went out for an early swim, returning to his nook before he would be visible from the air; but not on this day.

His wait was an exquisite balancing of instincts. Hunger was sufficient reason to start forth, and the pond's flow was a stimulation. The current, passing through the walls of the beaver house, divided around the Trout. All night its touch had slid along his skin, from nose to tail, as though he ceaselessly swam forward. Now he was awake to feel the fine strokes down his sides — the touch of moving water; only the sight of moving prey could be more quickening to a trout. But he submitted to the quieting urge. He stayed in his groove, with ears and lateral lines both listening for the hawk.

The fluffs of moonlight disappeared in a tremulous green shine. No wind rocked the surface now, but the Trout could see the current draining toward the dam. It was a checkered wavering, unhurried and unaltering. Daylight reached the bottom, where the water's ripples had been fixed in sandy silt.

Directly over him the Trout could look into the air. His view was circular, and small; his own length would have spanned it. Beyond that opening the surface was an opaque silver cover, stretching to the shores. Reflected in it were the floor of the pond, the swimming animals, and the underwater plants. The Trout could see the lustrous belly of a leopard frog spring past. He also saw, in the mirror spread above, the frog's bronze, spotted back. The pond was a shallow layer of the world, with a ceiling on which its life was repeated upside-down.

Upon the surface crashed a huge light-feathered breast. Claws reached and speared a bullhead. A brown throat, then a beak and eyes came through the top of the pond, and wings and tail. A shower of bubbles scattered downward as the long wings lowered in a sweep. The wings began to lift the Osprey. A final thrashing took him out of the surface, leaving the reverberations of his dive.

The wariness of the Trout released its check. He floated from his groove, still seeming motionless, as if the current had dislodged him. Slowly his fins commenced a ribbonlike stroke. His tail pressed gently on the water, left and right.

Freeing his entire strength in a tail-thrust then, he was across the pond. A spinning turn, and, energy closely held, he slanted toward the bottom silt — the touch, and a spasm of upward speed had flung him into the dangerous dazzling air.

A slicing dive back deep in the pond, a glimpse of another trout, and he whipped in its pursuit. But just before his teeth would have nicked its tail, he whirled, and the trout ahead whirled too, in perfect unison.

He cut forward in the channel of the current, throwing his tail from side to side as he tried to find in his own speed some full outlet for his strength. The water of the pond would give him nowhere more than a mild and yielding pressure. He was a native cutthroat of the Snake, a turbulent swift river, but the placid pond and little brook that fed it were the only home that he had known. In early summer of the year the beavers built the pond, his parents had come up the brook to spawn. The new dam trapped them and their offspring. The river poured along the east side of the marsh, so near that the Trout could feel its deep vibration. He had not seen it, but his spirit cried for its stronger flow, its more combative force.

Yet idle swimming could be pleasant. He glided to the backwash past the brook, toward food not scented, seen, or heard, but certain to appear. Sculled by his tail, he wove through bare elastic water-lily stalks, beneath a cover of translucent leaves. He was at rest in motion, fins outspread to ride the smooth support, his slippery skin quick-sliding through the wetness. But he stiffened, shot ahead, bent nose to tail, kicked back the tail in a sharp return, perhaps to savor the grace of a body incapable of awkwardness in an element incapable of angles: beautiful play.

He saw a streaming like fine grasses drawn by the current — dace! With a forward spring he snatched a minnow at the side of the school. Alarm flashed through them all, and the leaders swung to flee into the brook. The milling of the others would have made each one available to the Trout, but he swerved away.

He'd seen a pair of reedy, jointed legs, seeming to be rooted in the silt, but still, not quivering as reeds would in the flow of the pond. The dace swam toward them. The dace had left the safety of the shallows because a harmless moose was splashing there. The Trout had captured one, and now the great blue heron certainly would catch another. But would not catch the Trout! Already he was far beyond the stab of the bird's beak.

Near the shore the water swished with the feet of ducks. A quick look: no mergansers' feet, with paddle-toes for diving, there among the webs of mallards, pintails, and of baldpates. The Trout swam under them. He need not dread an enemy's unexpected dive here while the feet were moving the ducks about in search of food, while they were easy, pushing web-fuls of water back and folding in and drawing forward; not while one foot hung, a pivot, and the other swung an oval breast; or both of a duck's webs splashed at the surface, holding him bill-down. As long as no fear tensed the feet, the Trout felt safe.

The long stripe on a pintail's neck shone white as it lowered the bird's head, swanlike, to the bottom. But swiftly it was pulled above the surface. Now all the feet were quiet, spread from the feathered bellies, ready for a leap. The Trout, alert, poised in midwater.

He did not know what animal had frightened the ducks. While they continued their wary wait, the white keel of the pelican dipped through the surface, slid ahead, and, checked by its wide webs, glided to a stop. The Trout streamed off, away from the watchful ducks, and gradually forgot their warning.

When he was a young fish, nearly every animal he saw seemed hungry for him. One by one then he outgrew the threat of frogs, kingfishers, snakes, and larger trout. He learned the tricks of human fishermen. Minks and mergansers chased him still but could not capture him. No other creature in the pond was quite so swift. And he almost was too heavy to be carried by an osprey. Soon the Trout might reach security that few wild creatures know, unless the alien of the early morning proved a danger.

Every instinct whispers some command; for him the loudest command was always, *live*. He listened for it, always deferred his other urges to it. Survival was so strong an impulse in him that the most involuntary workings of his body helped him hide. The pale sheen on his belly matched the cover of the pond, to an eye below. One watching from across the surface might confuse the iridescence of his scales with scales of sunlight on the ripples. The black spots spattered on his skin disguised his shape when seen from any angle. To a mate or rival he might show two crimson gashes on his throat, but usually he folded them beneath his jaws.

When his alarm had quieted, he started to the beaver house. First he passed a bank of sedges. In summer when their shade was green, the Trout had turned to emerald here. This autumn day the grass was tawny, and its color, focused in his eyes, had caused the grains of yellow in his skin to scatter out and tint him olive. If the inborn guardian in his tissues could arrange it, he would live. Yet other animals also had ingenious aids, some useful in attack.

He circled the island on the dam, now moving through a tunnel of grasses, bent with the tips of the blades awash. The sun was laying gold bars over him. He moved with a little flourish, for it seemed that he was really safe. Beyond the far side of the island a floating log pressed down the top of the pond. He started under — and was circled with a crash.

Escape! Escape to a nook in the dam! He split the water and

was there. Wheeling, he shot in the hole and flung out his fins to check him. The water bulged in after him, as the one who chased him surged to a stop outside.

He had not seen what creature dived from the log. But his dash to the shelter, finished between heartbeats, was long enough to tell him that the other gained. Gained! Did panic echo, now, from days when the rush of most pursuers swept upon him like a wave?

His refuge was a space in the roots of a cottonwood, the dead tree anchoring the dam. Through interwoven fibres he could see his enemy, an animal he did not know, the Otter. The creature darted around the root-maze, trying to peer in. His eyes would show in one place, reaching for the Trout. A drive with a quick foot, and the brown-furred face would push into another hole. Eagerly it was weaving forward, cocked ears sharp as claws.

The Otter found a looser tangle, which his paws began to tear. The water was tainted with the scent of his excitement, acrid in the nostrils of the Trout. Close beside the Trout's face now a lean webbed paw had grasped a root. The claws were scratching as the toes kept tightening in convulsive grips. The Otter tried to burrow through, but the tangle held. Should the Trout attempt to reach the sturdier beaver house? No longer was there safety in a flight. He tensed his tail for a great thrust; yet he hesitated.

As suddenly then as if the Otter had seen a more accessible fish, he drew back out of the roots. He swam away with a vertical sculling, so that each roll took him to the top. The pulses in the water matched the surging that had stirred the pond at dawn.

The water beat for some time with his strokes and other creatures' startled movements. When the Trout could feel the light quick overlap of wavelets nearly spent, he knew that the Otter had gone to the far end of the pond. Then he could have fled to the beaver house, but he was waiting for the Osprey's midday dive. His new fear had not blurred his sense of the older menace.

The Osprey's perch was in the tree whose roots now hid him. He could not see the hawk, but when the spread wings glided from the upper boughs, they came into his air-view. He watched, as he never had from the beaver house, the way the Osprey hovered high above his victim, and how he plunged, so slanting his dive that he dropped from behind an unsuspecting fish. The Trout could recognize the jolting of the pond, the splashing as the Osprey struggled from the water, the sudden quiet, and widening of the echoes. The hawk returned in his air-view, carrying a mountain sucker to his branch. After he ate the fish, he flew back down to clean his claws. The Trout could see them cross the pond, thin hooks that cut the surface, trailing silvered sacs of air.

At last the water near the cottonwood roots sucked up, a motion meaning that some heavy animal was climbing out. A gust of drops fell onto the surface, as the creature shuddered the moisture from its fur. Feet ran over the top of the dam. As they passed the base of the tree, a sift of dirt fell through the roots and briefly stuck to the mucous coating on the skin of the Trout.

The pond was all in motion, for the wind had risen. The wind had stirred the marsh for several days, with short lulls.

The Trout sensed that it brought a change of season. He could even taste the proof of summer's end, as dust, seeds, crumbling leaves and bark washed through the pond.

Bright-edged shadows of the waves were racing over the bottom silt. They swept across the underwater plants and seemed to shake them. The surface layer of the pond was blowing to the upper end of the backwash. There the water turned below, to sweep back down along the bottom. Against the dam this flowing sheet rolled up. It pressed beneath the Trout's fins as a breeze will lift the wings of a bird.

Whenever the wind would strain the top of the rigid dead tree, he could feel a pulling in the roots. Abruptly they began to writhe, to tear. The Trout was out of the maze and back in the beaver house as if the water had parted for him.

The Osprey's tree, upturned by the wind, fell into the pond. Billows met rebounding billows, whirls and eddies struggled, surges rocked the Trout. Gradually the violence quieted. Through a cloud of mud he dimly saw that the trunk of the tree was under the surface, propped up from the bottom on its boughs.

He settled himself to feel the current's long touch on his sides. But what disturbing change was this: the water's stroking soon was regular, yet took a new course — not from his nose to tail but downward now. The water's pressure was becoming lighter and its color rosier. The top of the pond was falling.

Inherited memories warned him that the change was ominous. But he did not leave his shelter, for it seemed that a greater danger threatened him outside: the Otter had returned. Sometimes the Trout could hear him in the water, sometimes out along the narrowing shores. The Trout would not be caught through panic. He lay in his nook and watched the surface drop.

Only when it reached the nook itself did he nose outside. Feeling the Otter's surging near, he turned down to a refuge lower in the wall. The top of the pond descended on him there. The water, draining off the bank beside the house, was roily, so that he could not see where he would go. But he entered it and let its motion guide him.

The currents were not flowing in familiar paths. They all converged in a powerful new suction. Since the roots of the cottonwood tree had been interwoven with the dam, its fall had torn apart the beaver's masonry of mud and sticks. The whole marsh seemed to be swirling toward the gap and plunging through it.

The Trout turned back. He would escape to the brook. He sensed that he must leave the doomed pond and would seek the water's source, as many of the other fish had done. He could not reach it. While he, the one most wary, stayed in the house to escape the Otter, the pond had shrunk below the mouth of the brook. The only water now connecting them was a thin sheet crinkling over a pebble bar.

Gone, lost above the surface, were the undercut banks of roots, the grassy tunnels, brush, and other shoreline hideaways. The Trout returned to the lower end of the pond. He glided with his fins streamlined in the depressions in his sides, and with so slight a sculling that he might be trying to make smoothness hide him. As he approached the dam, he saw the Otter. Dodging up the bottom toward the island, he slipped beneath the log, which drifted now with one end resting on the silt.

The Otter was walking on the pond floor, moving with a

swing from his shoulders to his high arched rump. He somer-saulted to the surface for a breath; then looped and tumbled through the water. He straightened toward the hole in the dam. The fluent column of his body merged with the strands of the current, and he vanished.

The surface soon was shattered by a splash. The Otter was back. He had climbed up over the dam, beside the gap. He dived in, disappeared through the break, and again returned. A plunge, a joining with the water's sweep, and a swift ride: he had found a game.

The Trout was holding down his top fin, tense with fear. He spread it, and it struck the under side of the log. And yet his belly touched the silt. The log was the pond's last refuge, but the water soon would leave it.

Nothing in the Trout's experience could help him. He only could give himself to the urge that so intensely pressed to have him live. He waited until the Otter had dived and once more swung out through the hole. Leaving the log with a jet of speed, the Trout had reached the gap. A gushing force took hold of him. It hurled him through the break. Too quick for thought he dodged the wreckage of the dam. He leapt to pass the brink of the fall and dropped in the foam beneath. The cascade lightened, slowed, and he found himself in a shallow creek-bed, moving over cobblestones.

His high emotion quickened his choice of route: to the left, through streamers of emerald algae; right, along a slit between the stones; here a turn to miss a piece of driftwood, there to pass a boulder. The air was seldom far above his topmost fin. Sometimes he drew a breath of it, and it seared his gills with dryness. Avoiding one by one the unfamiliar hazards, he progressed.

His lateral lines were jarred by a new sound, a tremendous, heavy pouring. He swam around a bend in the creek and slid across a bar. And there a torrent plunged upon him, water more swift than any he had known. He was in the river, the violent tumult of the Snake.

It nearly overwhelmed him, but he found a milder flow along the bank. A curve there held a pool as in a shell. The pool was covered by a sweeper, a willow with its caught debris. The Trout discovered the refuge, entered it, and spiraled down into the cool green quiet.

Through the afternoon he stayed there, gaining back his poise and fitting his spirit to the strange new shape of his life. Most of the time he hung in the water, motionless, but now and then a ripple ran through his fins, and he chopped his breaths as with excitement. When the first gray wave of dusk washed over the pool, he rose to the top.

He swam along the bank, where ripples pattered into crevices among the roots. The motion of the water here was light and peaceful, like the pond's. Turning out, he met a crisper current, stimulating as the pond had never been. An even greater challenge growled from the center of the river, from grinding rocks that yielded to the push of water irresistibly strong. The Trout began to slant his strokes into the torrent. With a leap he sprang to the very heart of its taut pressure. Enormous weight bore down upon him, but he gripped it, driving his way against it with exultant power.

To fight! To fight the turbulent flow! To sharpen his nerves on its chill; to cut quick arcs through the weaving water; to throw so much force into his muscles' swing that they could drive him upstream, past the rocks beneath, with the whole

flood pounding toward him; to fling himself out into the air and see the river under him, a river wider than the pond, wide for his play — all this, the heritage of a trout, he knew now for the first time.

He faced the flood and, sculling exactly at the current's pace, remained above the same stone. Swirling past were many insects, blown in the river. He stayed to take a cricket only, for exhilaration sang in his nerves. He leapt —

But stopped, caught. Talons had stabbed into his flesh, were now locked through it. They were holding him in the center of a splash. A feathered throat was lowering before his eyes. Wings were sweeping down at the sides, enclosing him. The Osprey, forgotten in his conquest of the river, had made its sunset dive.

His torn nerves stung the Trout to action. The claws were powerful that bound him, but his thrashing bent their grip. They almost rigidly resisted, but they did bend. They were a pressure, like the river's force — to fight!

His instinct focused on one urge, to get himself in deeper water. Arching his body downward, he furiously tried to scull from side to side. The hawk's wings beat, attempting to lift his own weight and the Trout's. The wings and the driving paddle of the Trout's tail pulled against each other. So far the Trout had not been able to drag the bird down, but he held him under the surface of the water.

The river was aiding the fish. For the Osprey was growing desperate for a breath. At first the spines on the pads of his feet had pierced the skin of the Trout. They pressed their hold no longer. And the Trout could feel the talons in his flesh release their clutch. The hawk was trying to withdraw them, but their curving points were caught securely.

The bird and fish were swirling downstream. They jolted to a stop, snagged by the willow sweeper. The water's force was beating at them. It poured through the Osprey's feathers. The push of the wings was weakening. They suddenly relaxed, awash in the flow. And the claws were limp.

The Trout had fought another pressure, his exhaustion. When the straining of the talons ceased, he too relaxed. For long enough to gather a little strength, he waited. Then he began an intermittent thrashing. With bursts of effort he tried to jerk himself away. One by one the claws worked out, some slipping loose but more of them tearing through his sides. Finally a twist of his body sent him forward, free.

He turned down under the willow, lower and lower in the dark pool. With his flesh so cut, his lateral lines no longer clearly caught the echo of his motions, thus to guide him. He was careful therefore not to swim against the bottom. His chin touched, and he sank upon a stone. The stone was smooth, and soft with slime-coat algae. Soon he had drifted over on his side. His eyes were dull and his fins closed. His consciousness sank lower.

The Trout had been so stimulated by the river that he had ignored his innate caution. But now he was listening again to instinct, not to the water's roar. As he lay and waited for his strength to seep back into him, no creature could have been more passive, none more acquiescent.

The water's cold had numbed the anguish in his severed nerves. It would draw his wounds together. Already it had put in winter sluggishness the parasites that possibly would enter his exposed flesh. And gradually, as he rested, the cold became a tonic to his temper. Cold was as sharpening to him as the warm sun is to insects. By midnight he was swimming experimentally around the bottom. He circled higher. The Osprey was gone from the willow sweeper. The Trout moved out of the pool.

He found a backwash near the bank and held himself on the edge, where a smooth flow passed. Moonlight, falling on the surface, showed that a drift of small debris was swirling by. Drowned insects should be in it. His eye discovered a bright bit up ahead. He swayed forward. His mouth opened, touched it, and it broke with a singing snap. More came floating toward him — little round stars. Some winked out. He let the others pass.

But here was what he liked, a mayfly. Earlier in the day the year's last swarm had left the river for their brief erotic life. Now their delicate spent bodies would be nourishment for the Trout. Many others came his way. After his hunger had been satisfied, he took one more, and shot it out of his mouth for the chance of catching it again, of biting it in two and tossing out and snapping up the pieces.

Now he was not shaped like a smooth wedge, for the cover of one gill was hanging loose, and his sides were ragged. And so his balance in the turns of the water was not perfect. His fins were spread, all needed to aid his sculling tail. Yet the fins were rippling with an easy motion, easy as a creature can be only when it feels that more of living is ahead.

The winter, when a trout is quiet, would be long enough for his wounds to heal, and for his nerves to sharpen. Soon the last migrating Osprey would be gone — but would come back. And otters might be hunting here. The Trout must learn the dangers of this flood, and learn to be wary even while he was

exhilarated by it. He would. The wisdom of instinct, as of intelligence, can be disregarded, and it also can be drawn upon.

By the time he would be ready to try his strength once more
against the river, the Snake would be a slapping, dodging, driving, wild spring torrent.

The Osprey

✸

A flock of gadwall ducks rose from the marsh on pattering wings, pressed ahead slowly, began a turn; then were swept around at the wild speed of dry leaves blowing. To see their flight was to see the wind.

The wind showed, too, in the way the mallards floated among the pondweeds — all facing it as exactly as if it had swung them there. Most of the mallards had drawn their bills down on their breasts and pulled their eyelids together. A few tried resting the bills on their backs but soon had them forward again, for the wind reversed the feathers, changing the emerald heads of the drakes to black.

For five days the wind had unsettled the animals of the marsh. In the stirring depths of the pond the Leech probed and swayed from her hold on a lily stem. The Physa Snail, climbing the stem, whipped his shell. The Scud flounced about through a willow cove. Above these small ones the Trumpeter Swan was enclosing himself no longer in quiet.

Other animals, with practical instincts, sensed that the wind was bringing a storm, the end of the year's warmth and plenty. They were hurrying to prepare shelters. The emotion of the moose bulls surged to its autumn climax. Now they could not pass a brittle tree without horning off branches, or cross a trail without lowering their heads to scoop the bare earth. Their antlers clanged above the light running of Cottonwood Creek, the river's surging, and the side-wheels splashed by the feet of ducks feeding underwater.

The Osprey was one of the last to be disturbed. At morning, noon, and sunset he would take a fish from the pond. The rest of the time he perched on the top of a tall dead tree. The wind pried into the tight-layered down of his breast. It parted his tail. The hawk neither stiffened against it nor yielded his stillness to it. He stood without moving, while his eyes grasped into space as if the eyes were claws, taking nourishment from the sky.

On the fifth day of the wind the terrible strength of those eyes turned upon the animals of the marsh. The Osprey shifted at each forlorn call of a cow moose, at the kingfisher's clatter, at the slashing of a trout through the water. His restlessness sharpened into aggression. The swallows were exercising their wings for their fall flights — springing up, clapping the wings to their sides, and dropping in zigzag tumbles. The Osprey cried a warning clear and cold as a whistle. When the ravens flapped out from the black shade in the fir boughs, he chased them until their course veered up the river.

This was the Osprey's first autumn. He may have had no sure sense, yet, of the change he must make with the season's changing. On this day in September, however, the sky above Jackson Hole no longer seemed large enough for him. At least it was no longer large enough to share.

Head lowered between his shoulders, the Osprey watched

another hawk, a harrier, hunting over the marsh below. The Osprey unclasped a claw, then the other, moved an excited step on the branch. Many times that harrier had invaded his tree to challenge him, but the Osprey's parents always had been there to drive him out. For a week they had been gone. Sometime the young fish hawk must humble the harrier — on this day! Now, while the other one hovered over the Varying Hare.

Crying out his intention, the Osprey swung from his bough. Back came a jabbing of notes, raw and harsh. The harrier looped up with a facile speed, gained the higher level, spread his talons, and plunged for the Osprey's back. The Osprey shot from under him, wheeled, and spiraled over the harrier. His was the swifter flight, but the other hawk had the swifter instinct for a combat. The harrier gave himself to an eddy of wind, rose with it, turned to face the oncoming Osprey, drained the last lift from the gust, and passed on the upper side. As the two met, he raked a claw through the Osprey's wing. The Osprey banked to drive back at him, but the harrier broke from the fight at his instant of victory. He sank away and began to torment a trumpeter swan. The Osprey returned to his tree.

Both these young hawks had been hatched on the marsh and were growing up to occupy it together. They might have lived there in peace, for they were not competitors for the same food. But the harrier never needed a real cause for a conflict. He chased any hawk, including other harriers. He chased his prey when he was not hungry. These were play pursuits. Through them he had become a skillful captor.

The Osprey's foraging did not require expertness in chasing. It called instead for occasional concentrated power of muscle and nerve. Therefore he had wished to avoid the wearing, indecisive encounters that the harrier started — until this day when he was trying to clear his sky of other birds.

There was discord in the very style of the two hawks' flight. The harrier still was out and seeking his prey, but he appeared to be more absorbed in his contest with the wind, a strength as fierce and elastic as his own. He never forced his way against it, never farther than grace allowed. He swept to the center of its flow, in which he faced it and rode at one fine point in space as a trout will stand against onrushing water, while the wind spun on the edges of his feathers; but it lowered him in a lull, only to strike him with a blast that swung him up and over so that the pearly lining of his wings shone to the sky; yet he righted himself and made the curve a circle, descending on top of the air stream, soon sliding off to the side, to his roost on a tussock, over which he fluttered, briefly giving the wind its way, letting it toss him like a wisp of down in a column of heat; then, seeming as tireless as the wind itself, he swerved away to soar over the sedge beds.

Down through the angular boughs of his tree the Osprey followed every sway of the marsh hawk's wing. Its flight looked as soft as a moth's. The Osprey lifted his own wings above his back, slowly, seeming to stretch. The wings curved outward. He was off the branch, as smooth a drop as if he had launched into still air. With a measured pacing of wingbeats he crossed the pond. This was no play flight. The fish hawk mastered the wind. At the far end of the beaver dam he hung at treetop height, eyes turned down, searching the pond. He soon saw a mountain sucker swim toward a bend in the dam.

The Osprey collapsed the muscles that held him aloft.

Steeply he plunged, feet dropping and wings thrown up. His dive was veered by the wind, but he had allowed for the drift. His breast struck first. The blow shocked even his bones, but in that instant his right claw clutched the fish.

The green heaviness of water closed in front of eyes made to look through light. Water began its downward pull on the body built to fly. The hawk must act quickly to escape this enemy element — and quickly did. His wings gripped down, slowed, stopped his descent, began to lift him, broke the surface, and with a lively shedding of spray raised bird and fish into the air. As the Osprey skimmed over the pond, he shook the rest of the moisture from his feathers with a broken ruffling.

He held the sucker so that its head streamlined into the wind. To control its flapping, he placed one claw before the other, his outer toes down and the spines on his soles gripping into its scales. He closed his talons into its flesh, into its bones and heart, until the points of the talons came through. Before he had reached his perch, the sucker was quiet.

Releasing his hind claw, the Osprey alighted on it. The other claw came down, and he stood upon the fish. He did not start to eat it. He drew himself erect, and composure settled upon him as neatly as his mantle of trim feathers. His eye sought the harrier, still weaving above the marsh.

The harrier had discovered a mountain chickadee in a willow bush. The chickadee tried to dodge away, but the marsh hawk covered the bush, gliding forward and sliding back on the wind, hovering, tilting, swinging, leaving only far enough to give the chickadee hope and then dropping upon it, but not clutching it as long as the bird had strength to prolong his amusement. When the harrier finally took it, he ate it at once.

He found and grasped a meadow mouse, tearing the first warm bite from its back the instant the mouse's struggles eased into limpness. Perhaps there was not time enough in the harrier's day for a decorous wait after each killing; since he usually caught smaller prey than the Osprey did, he must catch more of them. The harrier had captured and eaten two victims, returned to his roost, and preened in the time that the Osprey must wait before he bit into his fish.

He moved his bill upon it. Back and forth on the cold skin slid the point. Either he was seeking a place to break the flesh, or testing to find whether the last reflex jerking had quieted in the dead nerves. Finally he made a neat cut in the sucker's shoulder, smoothly pulled until a piece came free, and tossed his head back to throw it into his throat. When he had finished the fish, he flew down to the pond and sped along the surface, trailing his feet until they were clean. He went back to his perch, and his eyes turned below, upon the indigo channels in the burnished bright grass and willows. If he searched for the harrier's brown tail, with its white arc at the base, he failed to find it.

At the passing of noon, the wind started to drive with all its force — this was a climax. The aspen boughs streamed from one side of their trunks, compelled to violate their delicacy of movement. Lead-blue ripples broke against the white sides of the swans. Many of the animals felt that this was the storm. Each in his refuge had pushed out his fur or feathers until he was as round as the very young of his kind.

The marsh was having its final scouring, and a whole new cloud of bark chips, leaves, and seeds had released their holds, were letting themselves be carried away. Should the Osprey give up his own hold, on his roost, his marsh? Should he yield to the urgency that was in him, let it take him wherever it might? Was the impulse strong enough, yet, to dislodge him from Jackson Hole?

At the top of the cottonwood he stood full in the wind's path. The beavers who made the marsh had used the tree as a pier, anchoring their dam into its roots on both sides, killing it by gnawing into its trunk and forming a pond against it. Isolated now within the living trees that encircled the marsh, it caught so much of the wind that on this day the Osprey would find it easier to soar than to perch.

He opened his wings, bent his heels for a push — and felt the bough sink away as if he had pushed the whole tree off balance. As he rose, the tree swayed. It began a downward plunge, slowly, then faster, with a tearing as the dam pulled out, and a geyser of spray and a roar when the tree struck the water. Its large branches held up part of it, but the trunk went under. Waves billowed to the end of the pond. Around the tree itself the water swirled. Broken twigs and boughs began drifting away toward the current now pouring through the break in the dam.

Startled wings rose from the marsh as the ducks, pelican, great blue heron, and numberless birds from the willows sought safety in the air. They all fluttered, the great wings slowly, the small ones shimmering among them, with movements through the flock like the eddies in smoke. Many terrified voices clamored, but the mice, shrews, and frogs had fled into hiding and there trembled, silent. A cow moose leapt the bank from the pond. A muskrat dived. The Osprey saw the Trout make a quick, slim trail to the tangled sticks of the Beaver's lodge.

The harrier was out, sweeping among the other birds. Since he was the more familiar danger, some of the small ones found themselves by fleeing from him back into the thickets. Looking down from above them all, the soaring Osprey saw his old nest, lying in the water like a ragged beaver house. He had known no other home except that nest and the perch beside it; at the end of a day or a flight he never had alighted anywhere but in the cottonwood. Yet he had a temporary home in the sky.

He left the confusion at the marsh, and his wings, beating in clean shallow curves, carried him upward. Their limber tips trailed on both rising and falling strokes, but there was a fine tension in the muscles that took him aloft with directness. Finally he stopped and rode the wind.

Dark blue clouds with crisp edges of shine spread above the peaks and obviously beyond them. He never had seen clouds like those before; they gave a new breadth to the sky. The Osprey did not have the kind of intelligence to measure horizons, but he may have sensed for the first time that a world existed outside this closed valley that whimsical human beings have called a hole. This was still the day when the valley had cramped his flight.

The Osprey knew clouds intimately. During his first weeks their passing had been the only movement that he could watch. No twig bent over the nest; nothing was above the young hawk but the white breast of his father or mother, and the clouds. He could see the mist form as hoods on the Teton peaks, pull away slowly, finally drift free. The clouds would move over him, as unhurried as his growing, and out of sight beyond the side of the nest where the guardian parent stood. They would seem faster when they came behind the white-feathered head with its band of purple-brown through the eyes, that masked the intensity of the eyes a little; behind the white breast and the brown shields of the folded wings.

The young bird moved even less than the adult ospreys. When his father brought a fish, his mother bit off pieces and gave them to her offspring. He had no cause for impatience; he was the only nestling, since two other eggs had been removed by a raven. But a quiet like that of clouds was in his nerves.

In early July, when he was a month old, he had crept to the edge of the nest. He had found then the base for his sky. It was an oval plain, almost as level as a lake. Even the valley floor was in the sky, but the circling mountains lifted to a white rim so much higher that it might have been a world's end. In Jackson Hole space was made real and immense by the walls surrounding it.

The sheer-sided basin was a valley to please an osprey, for all these hawks are attracted by heights; everywhere they build their nests on the tallest trees or near enough so they can perch on them. Below they must have the shine of water, shot with the glint of fish. The Osprey had found that, too. His nest was out on the valley floor, and water was all around it. A crease down the plain, choked with trees, led the Snake River past, here dividing around an island. And flowing in from the Grand Teton, the Great Breast, came Cottonwood Creek, cloudy with glacial milk. In the angle between the creek and the river, the beavers had formed the marsh.

As the infant Osprey had looked down and discovered the marsh, something had touched to intense life his eyes' liquid flame-colored depths. The pond may have suggested food. Or a glimpse of the harrier may have stirred some instinctive resentment. That young hawk, hatched only a week before the Osprey, had left his nest. Since the nest was built in the grasses, he simply had walked out of it. But on that day he already was trying to fly. Even in those early attempts he held his wings in a harrier's lovely up-sweeping arch. There was a restless grace in his sallies among the blown willow withes.

After this view of his wider home the Osprey had hunched back into his nest for another month. He had walked on the elbows of his wings, as well as on his feet, for he could not lift the wings. They had grown faster than the rest of him. At full size they would be half again as long as the harrier's, though the two hawks would have the same body length.

The first time the Osprey had trusted himself to his wings, and when he closed them for his first plunge into the pond, those instinctive actions were easier because he had, in his parents' flying and diving, an image of what he must do. But nature had a third great requirement to make of him and, this time, would give him no example. He faced now one of the hard conditions of being an osprey. Most kinds of hawks start on their fall migration in flocks of all ages, but the young Osprey did not even see his parents depart. They were gone one morning, leaving him with no hint that he must set out from this only home he remembered, with no directions, and no warning to keep the gleam of water always in view.

He had not been soaring long, on this afternoon in September, when the wind failed. A soft dampness was coming into the valley. Now he must beat his wings to stay up. Still he circled, crossing and recrossing the river, swinging out over the plain toward the mountains, east and west. The slopes were moss-dark; the plain was the color of wet stone. But the sun slanted through one break in the clouds, to touch a strip of the sage with a lustre so fresh that the earth seemed to shine with its own light, with the delicate brightness of things seen in farewell.

All the world that the Osprey knew was shadowed by change. His tree lay fallen. Southward the river showed a way out of Jackson Hole. Yet so far the hawk must have sensed only the restlessness which had aggravated his conflict with the harrier. For, when he tilted the planes of his wings to descend, he directed his flight again to the marsh.

The marsh looked strange. The water had drained from the side channels, which now were muddy troughs with banks of exposed, white, matted roots. The willows seem to be propped on other, inverted willows. The upper end of the pond itself had sunk away, leaving a basin of slushy silt. Water still lay in the lower end, but its level had dropped so that the door of the beaver house was revealed.

He hovered above the beaver house, peering into the sticks at its base, home of the large Trout, as he knew. A scream — the harrier's — struck from his left. It broke into short notes, hard as slaughtering blows. The Osprey sheered toward his attacker. The two would have met over the shore of the pond, but the Osprey went into a dive. For up from the brush, with an airy deadliness, swung another hawk, the young harrier's mother.

Checking his plunge, the Osprey skimmed under them. They turned in a down-curve so steep they were flung half-over, and straightened, and pressed ahead. Their light-bodied flight was now sharp and direct. The Osprey led into the cottonwoods separating the pond from the plain. Unerringly he chose spaces wide enough for his wing-spread, the length of a man's arm-spread. The margins were narrow, but sure. For the harriers

they were wider. Safely thus guided, they flew as fast through the branches as he did. He tried to lose them by weaving among the boughs. But the harriers, pursuers of dodging prey, seemed to foresee his moves. Their screams were upon him. They were short-cutting now.

An osprey is the most fearless of all hawks in defending its nest, but, unless its young are endangered, it is like other wild creatures: flees from a hopeless combat. The Osprey could not possibly chase off two harriers. He tried to prevent them from driving him out of his marsh but found finally that he could escape only in a long level flight. He swung away up the river. The harriers knew as quickly when they had lost. Behind the Osprey their cries grew faint; then ceased. The Osprey turned down again and stopped on the island across from the marsh.

Something white dropped on the branch beside him. Fiercely he held it still, by the strength in his eyes. He unclasped a foot, lifted it, sprang it upon the white one; then gripped with a life-draining grasp, so quick, so intense that his victim did not stir. After a pause he freed his talons, caught in the bark, lowered his head, removed his claw, and peered down to see the limp body. Nothing was there.

At once his head was erect, and his eyes defied the surrounding space. He discovered that many of the white flakes were falling. They tumbled and swirled, a cloud in fragments, a cloud of vagrant, disordered white scraps, spinning, staggering downward, each at its own pace. Between them the air looked gray.

Soon the mountains had vanished behind a nearer wall. The plain was becoming white, seen through a web of white boughs. Broken white movement wrapped closer and closer around the

Osprey — snow, clean, cold, unalive. On the opposite bank of the river he could see the marsh willows, now misty gold sprays. Besides these, nothing remained that had made this place home. The Osprey faced the breakup of his world without shrinking. Everything else might fall into soft, white pieces; the hawk even would hold astonishment back from his eyes.

Late in the day hunger drove him out of the island tree into the snow. With the accents of his wings still definite and controlled, he was across the river and the willows. He stayed low enough to keep his landmarks in sight, and flew toward the pond. But there no longer was much pond. A muddy hollow had a rivulet draining the center.

He searched in the rivulet for fish. None was in it. The equinoctial wind, the loss of his tree, the snow, the emptying of the marsh with his food supply: all these related incidents were nature's hints, which must serve now instead of his parents' guidance. The Osprey flew from end to end of the desolate new swale, turned then abruptly toward the river.

He never had caught a fish in the river. He had seen his parents do it, but even they had preferred to take their food from the pond. Knowledge inherited by his nerves sent him to the center of the current, where he discovered a whitefish. It was driving upstream by adjusting its fins to the flow, somewhat as a bird sweeps into the wind by tilting its wings upon the pressure.

Keeping the fish in sight, the hawk spiraled upward. To drive himself deep enough into the water, he must begin his plunge at least from treetop level. But when he reached that height, he could not see the fish. Everything below him was blurred by the snow. He glided down, assured himself that the prey was there still, climbed, and lost him. An osprey would not eat any-thing but a fish, one taken alive from the water. He would not even retrieve a fish that he dropped on the ground. A prolonged snowfall would make his kind of hunting impossible. When the frost-line moves down from the north, therefore, an osprey must go south of it. Did he need further hints?

Through the rest of the afternoon he perched on the island. The cloud of snowflakes thinned; then, with nothing to make its end noticeable, was gone. The horizon widened, not quite to the edge of the plain. A gray density still hung overhead, but high in the west it dissolved suddenly, and the Teton peaks appeared. On their rocky pinnacles was a crisp new marbling of white. The saddles now swung from summit to summit in smooth white loops. Beyond them the space was brushed with an opal light that foretold the end of day.

The Osprey would try again to catch a fish in the river. He flew upstream and back, frequently dipping for a closer view as he mistook the water's braiding for the flash of scales. The flow was so rapid that he scarcely could steady his gaze upon it. Nothing retarded this river; nothing broke it into foam. With the weight of mountain torrents behind it, it poured evenly over a bed of cobbles, slick with algae. The movement had a look of swift brutal force, a capturing pull.

But soon the Osprey found a Trout. This one was poised at the edge of the current, where the flow passed the quiet water enclosed by a curve in the bank. Smaller fish, insect larvae, and other trout food would be swirled along that line. The Trout was waiting for the river to bring them to his mouth.

The Osprey beat his way higher, took his position above the

Trout. Then he flung up his wings and made his steep strike. He caught the fish with both claws, sank until he was wholly submerged, and was drawn out into the current. He never before had felt its power. It enclosed him in tumult. But the river was water, like the pond. His wings knew what to do. They swung downward, and the hawk's dive was stopped.

He had not yet broken the surface when the wings, clutching together under him, reached their lowest point. The wings came up and began to beat. But opposed to their lifting was the drag of the river. And the Osprey had caught too large a fish, in his inexperience, adding too much to his weight. The Trout was trying to drive into deeper water. Its thrashing had locked the Osprey's talons into its bones. Again the long wings drew together below the hawk, but he did not rise to the top of the water, not high enough even to snatch a breath.

As he struggled, he was swept toward the mouth of Cottonwood Creek. Just above that point a dead willow, drifting down, had caught on the bank. Half-submerged, it floated there securely. The Osprey struck on the sweeper, was held against it briefly, was pushed out by an eddy, seemed to be swinging away, but was stopped again when the longest branch slid beneath his half-opened wing.

Now the clean, brown and white bird was wreckage among the muddy leaves, grass, and twigs snagged by the willow. When one of the current's cradles reached him, the soaked feathers of his head rose above the surface but at once were submerged again. The Trout wrestled in the loose claws. Torn but alive, it worked itself free. The Osprey did not know. As soon as his talons were empty, they folded in, limp. The ripples began to slap one inert foot against the branch.

The harrier discovered the Osprey. Swinging along the bank in his hunting, he glimpsed the white head in the water's sweep. His sharp, high scream was like talons piercing. The cries that followed might have been the attacks of a ravenous beak. That was always the cadence of the harrier's taunts — a shrill threat breaking into impatient gibes. The Osprey had heard it many times.

The closed eyes did not open, and the claws of the Osprey did not twitch. But the wild ones are not deceived about death. The harrier must have sensed that under the numb brain of the fish hawk some valor of flesh was fighting. Though he could not enter the water, the harrier continued to strike his enemy with his voice.

That voice had roused the energy of the young Osprey each time that it stirred his parents to a chase. Twice that very day, the sound had stimulated a surge of anger in him, and therefore a surge of strength. The harrier might more nearly have defeated his rival if he had flown away, silent, leaving in the Osprey's ears and the depths of his spirit only the vast indifference of the water's roar.

But he remained, screaming, above the willow sweeper. And then once when the Osprey's claw struck the bough, it took hold. It lost the hold but found it again. The next effort the Osprey made was to reach for the same support with his other claw. Slowly, pulling one above the other, the feet lifted the great wet bird until he was out of the water and up in the willow's clustered boughs, above the river.

He rested there with his wings spread and his feathers fluffed to dry. A weak shake, another more vigorous, rid the feathers of some of the water's weight. Between these attempts the Osprey was quiet, gathering and pointing his energy, a skill practiced many times before dives.

The harrier still tormented him, but not so constantly. That hawk was watching for some careless creature to expose itself on the empty canals of the marsh. Various homeless animals had prowled there before the snow fell. The harrier, hoping for more of them, was forgetting caution.

The instant came when the Osprey's wings could lift him. He stretched and lowered them several times; then hovered over the willow, not quite secure. He crossed to the island. His next exercise was a flight up the island shore.

The harrier was gliding over the river, just lower than the tops of the bank willows, peering among them to a bay in the thickets. Now he was facing downstream. From the island's northern tip came the Osprey, riding the river-wind, sweeping toward him with motionless wings. When he was near, he cried a warning, and the harrier swerved but not quickly enough. The Osprey dived upon him, and a blow from his claw on the harrier's head sent the harrier reeling over, stunned. He hit the water. Instantly it snared his capsized wings. With no chance to right himself, the harrier was carried down on his back into the tumbling currents where Cottonwood Creek joined the river.

The Osprey flew a short way along the bank and alighted on a snag for a further rest. As he waited, his ears were touched by a sound that was new. It came from upstream and was like a distant reaching cry. As it approached, it fluctuated into numerous voices, clear and urgent, the voices of Canada geese, midway on a long journey. All had the same uncertain, searching tone. Could these voices, anywhere, ever mean, *This is home?*

The Osprey's eyes found the geese, flying in a long thin line with a forward point near the center. The line swung at the river's bend, its inner side consolidating, the outer side widening. Coming on again, both sides straightened, rippling from the point to the ends. The line seemed one, as the voices had, but when it came closer the waver of wings made it many.

As the geese beat their way toward him, the Osprey could see the black feet pressed beneath their tails. The long necks stretched ahead, and the level bills strained toward some remote goal. The geese were above him. Then they were a little beyond. Seen from behind, the flock pointed more sharply. It was like the outline of a single bird, pushing south. The voices were lighter now, trailing their call.

The Osprey raised his wings and glided out off the branch. He circled once over the snag and, finding his steady, smooth rhythm, started down the river behind the geese. At the end of the valley the flock turned eastward around a butte and disappeared. The Osprey flew on without them. He needed no other guide but the shine of water below, and he had that. The river led through a pass, out of Jackson Hole.

Beyond, he found the wider world. It seemed full of movement beneath him, for the mountain ranges rose one against another like waves, crested ridges and valley troughs, as far as he could see.

A tint of gold touched a low edge of the overhead clouds. It was pale, but the clean shade that promises brighter color. The rays pierced up through a westward canyon. They reached more of the clouds. Soon there was flame in the non-living universe, fire on the polished rock of the peaks, and the vapor. The fire and vapor were all in motion.

The Osprey flew into sunlight, the sunlight that was swinging south. At the end of winter again he would follow it, and it would bring him north, once more to his Teton marsh.

In the Willow Cove

THE MOSQUITO
THE SCUD

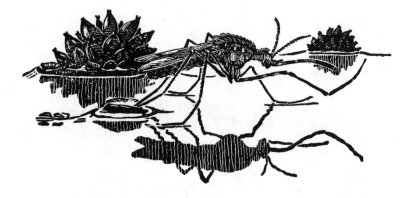

In the drift at the shore of the willow cove were pricks of movement. The drift itself was lifeless — broken twigs and yellow soaked leaves; soon they would be brown trash on the pond floor. But a bubble has broken near a piece of floating bark. A caddisworm dislodged it. There an ice-gray bit has disappeared: the startled Scud, unnoticed till he vanished. A speck of shadow, like a small black seed, is darkening the crotch of a cottonwood twig. The morsel, the Mosquito pupa, is recovering from a breathless flight, a dodging through the water to escape a salamander.

Never had the Scud and the Mosquito been so safe as now. In the last few days the wind had blown up through their bay this raft of leaves and sticks. It was a tangle of tiny nooks. Until it came, a stalk of pondweed was almost the only shelter.

The shore was a crescent of bare mud here. At its northern point the roots of a willow gathered into a knot that branched up into stems. A pupa could have hidden among the roots, but a snake too often rested there. At the south point grew a stand of bur-reeds. The narrow leaves pierced through the surface in the shallows. Farther out they floated, penciling off with a stiff grace, toward the dam on quiet days but now swung toward the backwash by the wind. Young fish lay among them, streamlined bodies hard to see in the fine-barred shade. The Mosquito had had to find concealment from the snake and fish within the flimsy pondweed. And then the wind deposited the saving drift.

In the two days since her latest molt, the Mosquito had wanted desperately to be ignored. Her life had reached some kind of climax. She had molted four times during the few weeks since she cut her way out of her eggshell. The first three molts she had emerged in about the same shape, only larger — a small gray larva torso, very lively, with a hairy body, a black head, and a tail from which a breathing tube branched off. She still felt like the same Mosquito after the fourth molt, for she had the same nerves, but she was a different form now, heavy at the top, with a flattened abdomen curled under. Odd new structures, packed around her like an inner coat, had begun to grow. It seemed that her skin would burst at once, it felt so full.

In other ways her life had changed. Until two days ago the satisfactory thing had been to eat. Sometimes she hung at the surface, caught on the film by the tip of her breathing tube. She was upside-down but whirling the brushes on her face to send a stream of tinier animals and plants into her mouth. The motion of the brushes was so vigorous that it moved her over the top of the cove. At other times she fed on the pond floor, still with her tail-end up as she bit off specks of the ooze or brushed them in. In either place she had been an energetic little body, seldom resting.

Food meant nothing to her in her present stage. This was a time to be quietly secret: strange for one who had been so active, yet she did as her new needs were directing.

Leaning passively against the floating twig, she could look

about. The eyes she had had as a larva could distinguish only light and movement. The new, more complex eyes she was developing may have shown her shapes — and redness. See the brilliant tongue of the garter snake that hangs so close above her from the willow. See the spinning bloodworm. See — oh, *see* — the scarlet on the throat of the trout. If he sees *her*, she never will escape to the air above.

The Mosquito waited, giving her energy to the transformation taking place inside her. But during the afternoon her peace came suddenly to an end. Ripples swelled across the cove. And now she sinks in a swirling vortex as a webbed foot pushes down above her.

The pelican was wading through her cove. The silt he stirred up clogged the gills of some of the underwater creatures, killing them. The Mosquito pupa flipped about, erratically darting, as she tried to find a refuge.

His final surging washed her in among the willow stalks. The snake was gone. And no breeze entered the close-grown willow. The water of the miniature lagoon was just what water should be — quiet wetness in which to lie and grow. Shadows stained it to a darkness the Mosquito matched; no enemy discovered her. But if she felt that she could stay, she was mistaken.

Her bounding had strained her fragile envelope of pupal skin. No sooner was the water leveled than the skin split down her back. Ready or not, she must begin her life in the air.

Her abdomen stretched back along the surface, and her head and chest came out of the split, for the first time into the world above the pond. She took a great breath, filling the air-tubes meshed through her insect body. It swelled her out, and her skin more widely opened. Legs flexible as hairs unwound from around her shoulders. The first pair pulled themselves free, stiffening at once. Their folds unbent.

With a look of slow, experimental wonder the Mosquito laid one foot on the water. She put the other down. A middle pair of legs came out and lowered, and a hind pair. On her sides had been two flattened sacs, and from them now she pulled out — wings! Up from their veins and edges when they dried would stand exquisite iridescent fringes. From beneath her chest a beak swung forward; and her abdomen slid from its outworn sheath. She found a slippery stand on the surface, rested on her feet, and waited. She was a real Mosquito now, though very pale and still too soft.

If the pelican had come plunging back, she would have drowned. The least breeze, even ripples caused by a jumping trout, would have tipped her over. She seemed too delicate for a world so hazardous and rough. But none of the violent things that could have happened did.

One by one she held her feet in the air to dry. When they had hardened, she dared to take a few steps on the film. She reached a willow stem and lifted a foot against it. The foot stuck; she had claws! She climbed the stalk a short way, stopping with her claws caught into the bark. Never in the water had she felt a thing so solid. Her body had touched the plants and the pond floor, but she had had no way to grip them.

She stayed on the stem until her tissues stiffened and her color changed to brown. But her eyes were nearly blinded by the shine here. As the sun went down, the pond became more glaring. The floating bur-reeds held the dazzle on their flat wet blades, and the water-lily pads were discs of light.

Hungry dragonflies were hawking up and down the shore. Their wings were brittle-bright and rattled as they beat. Instinct may have warned the Mosquito of new dangers in the dry-land world; she may have felt uneasy at the dragons' clatter. Or possibly her own wings simply opened and began to whir when they were firm.

Their fanning swung her off the stalk. She did not move across the air, as the dragons did, but up and down as she had bounded from the bottom to the top of the pond. Gradually she flitted up through the willow, higher with each wavering vibration. But she found no film above the air to which she could attach herself and float, as she had clung to the water's film.

She fluttered down, away from the shore and over a watermeadow. The sunshine drained away, and she flew in the dusk more confidently. Ahead was a cluster of gleaming waxen drops, snowberries, obviously juicy. Some new impulse made her stop.

She alighted on a berry and pointed her beak to its skin. The beak had an outer sheath, which was elastic. She pushed it up and down. Within the sheath were four long blades with sawtoothed points, and a slim tongue. Several times she straightened the sheath and pulled it back along the blades. Those inside tools could fit together to form a tube. She thrust them into the berry. They were still too soft to do much cutting, but the berry skin was tender. They worked in far enough to let her pump out juice. It did not go to her stomach but to sacs behind her throat. She would keep her stomach empty till her hardened beak could pierce some firmer substance, from which it would drain a different, richer nourishment — what?

A chill was striking through the air, a threat to small things like mosquitoes. She lifted from the berry, hovered till she found a sheltered nook beneath the drooping head of a thistle. Moonlight spread across the meadow, silvering the night, creating a world congenial to an insect nearly as unsubstantial. Bats would be skimming prey, but dragonflies and insect-eating birds would not be out. This was a mosquito's time — but not her weather.

Perhaps she was the last mosquito to emerge from the pond this season. There never were many at this marsh. Fish were too numerous; they caught the young before they left the water. Most of those who did escape the fish had come out earlier. The Mosquito had seen no others in her brief time in the air.

In the morning, sunlight quickly warmed the meadow. She stayed in the thistle then because of the brightness and the breeze. Around her she sensed a multitude of new strange things. The Leopard Frog was sunning himself beside a stone. He had a look of life. She was not one of those mosquitoes who would like a frog's blood, but he evidently had possibilities that no stone had. The Varying Hare was nosing over a clover patch. At a sound the tall ears rose, high as the thistle-head. The ears would be a tubelike shelter, and had some other meaning, not yet understood.

Even nearer than the Frog or Hare were creatures more important to the young Mosquito. In the grass below the thistle lay a dried fur foot; for half the summer it had lain there. On this autumn day six male mosquitoes huddled under it. They did not know of her, nor she of them. Instinct would send them out to seek each other only in the dusk. These days the temperature went down with the sun, however, and they could not risk the cold.

But sometimes nature's great events bring benefits to the smallest creatures. The recent winds had been forerunners of the equinoctial storm. That vast disturbance reached the marsh soon after noon. Ahead of it dense layers of clouds rolled over the sky, so darkening the valley that any mosquito might mistake the twilight of the storm for the twilight of the day. And yet the noon warmth lingered on the quickly shadowed earth.

The male mosquitoes were deceived. They left their nook and flew above the willow. Moved by a last unlikely hope, they formed themselves into a little swarm. Six only, not a hundred or more, they whirled and swung together on the chance that female eyes would find them, and females hear the whine of their song. But how could so few send a call throughout the marsh?

One female heard it. She left the thistle, like a bit of the down herself, and with her airy, tossing flight rose through the twigends to the top of the tree.

She alighted on the highest leaf. The males have sensed her presence. Frenzied, they will drive their wings to their utmost speed. Their summons has become a twang. They have gathered in a closer living cloud, that sways above the tree. How can the female not be stirred by such a desperate dance?

She rose from the leaf, hung over it; then darted to the swarm. The six males closed around her. The boldest clutched her, and the pair fell, lightly tumbling, to the ground. In the grass below the tree they clung together, holding a long embrace for creatures so fine-spun and slight. They separated, the male with his destiny completed, the female with hers just begun.

In a drastic climate like that of Jackson Hole, instinct must be answered with a quick obedience; the time may be so short, the opportunities so few.

Swiftly the young Mosquito gave herself to a new obsession. She must find a certain kind of nourishment, needed to mature her eggs. Male mosquitoes live on the juice of plants, and so could she, but her eggs would develop best on a different sort of food.

All the scents around her suddenly became engrossing. To smell them, her antennae swung in one direction and another. They found the odor of the Frog's skin, of the snail shells left by a muskrat; found the clammy fragrance of the daisies, and many others, but not yet the one that will attract her.

Then — a wave of moose scent from the pond! The Mosquito flew out toward it, finally to the bay where two grown moose and a calf were resting in the shallows. The large bull was asleep. His fleshy nose, his muffle, stretched along the top of the pond.

The Mosquito came down on it. At once her beak began to work. She inserted the stylets in the short fur, to the flesh. With the blades held firmly in the sheath-end, she was sawing. Soon the blades were through the skin. On in they cut. The Mosquito lined her mouth-parts into a tube and started a pumping in her throat. A steady flow of the Moose's rich blood drained into her stomach.

Her saliva entered the Moose's tissues. Possibly it kept the blood from clotting; whatever its use, however, it stung the Moose's nerves. He tossed his head and dropped it into the water. The Mosquito could have drowned. But, startled by the movement, she withdrew her beak in time. She fluttered off as the muffle plunged below the surface.

She hovered before the bull Moose, waiting to take another drink of blood. If the marsh had been a world planned for mosquitoes, she might have spent the afternoon on the muffle. But the marsh was a home for many creatures — also for this dragonfly who sweeps out from the shore.

The Mosquito had no chance to dodge. The other did not give her time. Flying with her legs held forward, basketlike, the dragonfly surrounded the Mosquito with them. The pond, now quiet, mirrored that embrace, the quick uptilting of the dragon's body, brilliant blue and, as she flew away with her captured prey, the leveling of her shiny wings.

THE SCUD

If the Scud could have known that day was to be his last, he would have lived it just as he did. He scrambled about for food and tumbled through the water with such energy that he must have found most flavors and motions that he liked. He always seemed to have a giddy kind of eagerness, but on the day of the equinox he acted as if each pleasure snatched him from the last.

A new chill in the water brightened him. It promised winter, the good time, time when the plants took on the taste of sweet decay, when enemies were slower. Then a scud, his ways all quickened, lived more freely in the shadow of the ice along the shore. Perhaps his nerves remembered.

When he began the day, the only light was the moon's. It did no more than loosen the blackness in the cove. No matter; he never seemed to care where he was going. He flung himself back, forward, up, down, level, sidewise; the fun was in the wildness of the motion. When he landed with a bump, the water cushioned it. He jerked his tail up under his chin now, arching his back so quickly that he jetted out the water from between his fifteen pairs of legs. The spurt had sent him flying. With a little bounce he stopped against the surface film and let himself drift slowly down . . . but snapped together again, with a somersaulting, and the next jet threw him up to the top at a different angle. He thumped on something solid: food? Turned over with a flip, he reached and sniffed with his antennae. It was a tactile question — answered by *no*, for he found that he had hit a piece of driftwood.

A new plunge brought him up against the belly of a shrew. His feelers touched her velvet fur, and he darted off, escaping though his jointed shell, like marble tissue, shone a little in the moonlight. She could have seen him.

He brushed to a stop among the leaves of a pondweed. They hadn't the harshness of the leaves that fell from the shoreline brush and trees; the pondweed, like most underwater plants, was softening as it died. Gripping a stand with his climbing legs, the Scud pushed clawfuls of the rich food into his mouth. On the ends of his first four feet were tiny flaps, which he folded over to clasp the pondweed leaf as a human being clasps when his hand is in a mitten. Pondweed leaves were always limp and tender, but any scavenger would like them better now that they were ripe. The meal was giving a pleasant start to the Scud's last day.

A crumb of leaf came off in his claws. While he held it, nibbling, he went for another tumble in the water. First he rode by his backward bounding, but he had other ways to swim. He lay in the water, belly up, and sped along by waving his middle, swimmeret feet. He sank to the pond floor, made a forward snap, and when the jumping feet on his tail touched bottom, sprang, a push that shot him to the top. Could this be anything but play, a little acrobat performing while he ate?

Nature had given him four kinds of legs, with which he could go in every way but a walk. They were useful in reaching food and dodging captors, but they also could provide enjoyment. The liquid denseness of the water held him and yet yielded when he wanted speed. And so he flew through the cove with the swiftness that had earned his kind their lively name. Some early human, watching one of these half-sized shrimps, had called it a *scud*, the word for the blowing of foam from the crest of waves.

When the last of the leaf was gone, the Scud crawled up in the floating leaves along the shore. Here he would stay while the teeth between his stomachs ground his food still finer. And just in time! A school of little dace and trout, who had slept among the reeds beside the cove, had wakened in the brightening daylight. They glided out to look for food among the looser plants.

The trout were a special danger now at the end of summer. Earlier they had been too small to attack a scud; later they would leave the shallows. In September they were here and the size to plague a shrimp, to bite his legs off when they could not swallow the whole of him. A few lost legs would grow again, but if the Scud were injured badly, the fish would sense his weakness and, like a pack of little wolves, keep nipping him until he died.

How keenly the trout moved; even in flowing dreamlike through the reeds they were not careless, as the Scud was. One used a burst of speed to weave precisely through the pond-weed, coasting to a stop as the glossy thickness of the water slowed him. One searched across the mud, tail up and flickering when the fish found something good to eat. Another trout hung under the surface, making forward stabs to gobble water-fleas. To find their even smaller food, the fleas were bounding up and down as if on jerking strings. Trout also nibbled at the water-bloom, which the wind had crinkled in against the shore. It seemed but an emerald dust and yet was a world of furious minute activity.

The Scud was here in the debris because he liked seclusion while he rested; he was not smart enough to time the coming of the fish. In fact, there were hunters at the waterline. The Scud lay on his side with his climbing feet clasped onto a cottonwood leaf. A salamander floated near him in a trancelike sleep. One dainty hand on the stem was holding her, and she looked almost as delicate as the envelope of herself, her shed skin, drifting, perfect to each finger. But if she woke and saw the Scud, her back would stiffen in a twisted arch as threatening as a snarl. Her jaws would snap down over him, and she would shake him with ferocity.

Chance saved him from the salamander. But when he moved, his giddy course discouraged predators. Soon he flung himself out from the leaf — in any direction; he was sure to alight eventually on food. A garter snake was idling in the cove and watched him, but she did not strike. His way was too erratic. He darted through and around the legs of a great blue heron, and the heron saw him, but he was too wildly fleet a bite.

He let himself drop down to the bottom and began a hurried scrambling in the mud. It moved him sideward to a tiny twig. His jointed body curled around it, and his feelers urgently investigated. The end was hollow. Now the beadlike head of a caddisworm peered out. The worm had made the twig. It was his tube, an imitation of bark, composed of minute scraps of darkened leaves that he had glued together with saliva. He crawled forth, seeming a black-legged ant, and reared up over the edge of the tube. The Scud bent double with a snap that put him on the floor of the pond again, but out of the caddis' range.

Here too he scratched in the ooze. Perhaps he hungered for a certain food. Behind him was the nymph of a dragonfly, voracious creature. The nymph's clawed tongue was folded under her throat, and she could shoot it forward faster than the Scud could flee. She had seen him and was gliding toward him with the movements of her legs concealed in the ooze. But the Scud, in prodding about, turned just in time to see the smoothly advancing head. Motion was his warning! He was up in the water, shooting now into the reeds.

The fish were gone. Once more good fortune had favored his accidental landing. For three years luck like that had saved him. He did dodge anything he saw approaching, but he never had been able to distinguish between the threatening and the harmless objects, between a snake, for instance, and a branch that fell in the pond. The little water-fleas did not have even that much caution. Their leaping was a search for food, not ever a flight. The trout, on the other hand, were learning to recognize their enemies. Some day they would remember that a mink might chase them, but a muskrat never would. Such grades of instinct ran throughout the population in the pond. For instinct was no quality, like breath, that all had in a similar proportion. In some it was simple and in some complex. On this day it was tested. A catastrophe occurred, and whether a creature lived depended on how well instinctive habits helped him.

The happening was one familiar in every wilderness: a tree blew down. But this tree was a pier in the beaver dam. In overturning, it opened a wide gap, and the marsh began to drain away. Till now the pond and the bays that wound back through the willows seemed to belong here, to have been here for as long as the river rumbling past and the valley floor itself. But the marsh was the work of a single beaver family, and so temporary that one tree blowing over could return the place to the plain.

Its falling splashed an ominous wave into all the bays. The Scud had spent the latter part of the morning eating at the algae coating on the reeds. He was lying on the bottom, curled around an end of root, when the wave rushed in. It snatched him from his hold and swept him shoreward with a wash of loose things, wisps of ooze, the cast-off skins of insects, specks of silt and trash, and dizzy little animals. The wave smacked up against the beach and sucked out. But the Scud had caught on a pebble and stayed behind.

At first he was a full length under the top of the pond. The water dropped, but the surface film stretched up for a while; a peak in the liquid sheet still covered him. It broke, though, and he scrambled back down into deeper water.

He returned to the open cove and alternately ate and rested, with but two things strange: the outward drag of roily mud along the bottom and the shortening distance of his bounds between the pond floor and the top. Finally the shore and the leaf-drift that he knew so well were lost above the shrinking water-line. On the ooze was a small migration, nymphs of dragonflies and mayflies, leeches, snails, and caddisworms who dragged their cases with them. The tubes of the bloodworms were not movable. Some of the owners stayed inside and suffocated; others left the homes they had stuck together, grain by grain of mud, and swam out with their neighbors.

The Scud was near the forward edge of the swarm. Soon he had gone beyond the cove, beyond the reeds, and reached a stand of water-lilies. The strong round stalks had held up out of the surface, but they bent at last. The leaves and blooms were riding down. One after another, they had given the Scud a place to cling. When they came to the pond floor, he would stay among them until the water was very shallow; then bound on.

Finally he stopped in a small depression in the silt. It held a tiny pool. The water was trapped here and was sinking swiftly.

Some animals had known, or quickly learned, the importance of following a current. They went out with it. But the Scud was satisfied with his miniature pond. His instinct had been able to bring him this far, but it stranded him.

He lay on his side and waved his climbing legs in the water. His gills were on them, and their motion always before had sent new oxygen through his air-tubes. But soon his legs were waving in the air. Gills must take their oxygen from moisture. The Scud groped downward to the wetness on the silt but could no longer reach enough of it to cover him. His legs began to wave more slowly. And then he was quiet, one of many to whom the beavers had given a chance for life that now was gone.

In the afternoon the equinoctial storm brought snow. And early in the night a new pond started to fill the basin. For the Beaver was at work, repairing the dam. By morning the water lay above the Scud to a depth of several lengths. A bubble of air was caught between his forefeet. It started to rise and turned him over. Seeming to clasp his shining ball, he drifted up through the water, heavenward, looking like a light little animal soul.

The Mink

THE MINK

☼

The shine of the moon was spread like a thin snow on the openings in the forest. It showed that the berry bushes were topped by grass-heads, lately grown tall to give their seeds to the wind. They were giving them also to the animals. The grass quivered in sinuous streaks, as under it meadow mice hurried along their paths. They were all awake tonight, hunting for seeds of the reed-grass, foxtail grass, lupines, angelica. A storm, the arrival of winter, was due. And the mice would store food in their bodies as well as underground.

The scent of them poured, a foggy musk, down the bank of a stream. It had stopped the Mink, swimming past.

His nose easily followed the curves of the mice's runways. And a lightness came into his braiding gait as he sensed all around him the stir, the squeaks, and nibblings that promised chases. A trembling stalk, there ahead, flung him up in a bound, to alight with his teeth infallibly in a mouse's neck. Soon he had caught three, as they sped to their holes in what to them was a hastening but a scurry stupidly slow to the Mink. He laid the three bodies behind a stump.

A tour of the runways showed that the other mice, frightened, all had gone down in their burrows. The Mink could not squeeze himself into the holes. He stretched at full length, concealed by a flat spray of juniper, and watched for a jerk in the grass.

Hind feet were under his haunches, his forelegs spread to the sides. His chin was upon the earth, hiding its white spot. That spot was the only mark on his fur and could flash a warning to mice. All now that might shine, about him, was his eyes' glisten. They were almost exactly the shade of his purple-brown hair, but their intensity fairly sparkled.

As he peered out for victims, his eyes and his mouth were joined with a tautness somehow touching, a look of tension combined with the humbleness, the uncertainty, of a very young creature. The speed of his spring would be blinding; no mouse could escape. Yet with every reason for confidence, he did not have it, it seemed.

With a quick step-up beneath him, his hind feet had steepened the arch in his back. Then he straightened — leaping out through the grass, and no whip of a willow bough ever was faster.

The meadow mouse died with a few convulsive kicks and a sag into limpness. Even before the Mink turned with it toward the stump, its unwary life had become a tatter of fur. The Mink dropped it beside the others, not with a manner of satisfaction, but as if the prey, once caught, did not matter.

He added two more from the colony to his heap. Then back in his lookout, he let his eyes become lazy, and dozed. A deer mouse fled past without waking him — leaving her scent, though, a brighter strand in the meadow-mouse odor. The squealing of red-backed mice roused the Mink. Two were fighting behind in the fallen leaves. First they had jumped at each other; now they were fencing with forepaws, while their teeth sliced for holds. With two flashing pounces, the Mink captured both. Those, too, went behind the stump. And so did the deer mouse, trailed to her perch on an aster, where she was eating seeds.

Leaving the grass patch, the Mink returned to the stream. He moved down the bank with his walk heavy now, his tail stiffly held, and the hump of his back turning rigidly from the step of one short leg to that of another. His nose pointed earthward. It still found the scent of mice, mice everywhere. Their soft flavor, so soon satiating, had been the only taste in his mouth for too long. Of his store of them by the stump he had taken no single bite.

Below on a slim spit of sand he glimpsed a blotch of moist lightness, dark-spotted. Leopard frog? He sprang out, his body suddenly limber and graceful, to alight on an aspen leaf, yellow, black-mottled with winter's blight. Disappointments like that had become familiar. Beyond was an idling flow, polished by moonlight He threw his strength into a sweeping stroke, for upon the bottom he saw the spread shape of a frog, a real frog undoubtedly. It lay motionless, pearly belly and throat uppermost, its legs tensed for a kick into the life now lost. Taking it in his mouth, the Mink swam to the water's edge, where he lay on a pad of mud, eating the frog, dead to begin with and caught without combat.

Oh, where were the live frogs? The Mink sped away on his search, downstream, below the roots undercut by the current. His running was swift as a bird flight, the naked soles of his feet finding touches on snags, rocks, and driftwood, a pattering

P&G MATTSON

quick and smooth as the tracing of wing-tips. Once he did sense the bitter odor of frog, but it was faded. He paused at a moss-cap and a pebbly crevice where he had found frogs all summer. Now his glance strained into emptiness.

Frogs had provided much of the movement the Mink delighted to stop. The tadpoles would float up, strike the surface, break into wriggles that drove them down, drift to the top again; and once more burst into action. But the Mink had ended their routine, sometimes eating them, often content merely to make them still. The cricketlike small frogs, later, had amused him. When two danced around each other, eyes full of fight and mouths gripping the ends of the same worm, how quickly he finished their conflict! The older frogs had spent too much time squatting motionless in their crannies. They refolded their legs, however, at any small stimulus, a gathering of alertness that might shoot them out into the brook, under its silt, a challenge to any mink's swiftness. For all of his half year of life, on every stream that he traveled, the Mink had found numerous frogs. But for four days, now, he had not seen one that was living. Why? Where had they gone?

His hunt on this night was not only for frogs but for any leaping, gliding, swimming creature — especially for fish. He left the mud, dived in the flow, and began to search in the pools where young cutthroat trout had tried formerly to evade him. He was a looping, curling swing of dark motion through the shaded and moonlit eddies, through the depths which ought to be shot with dodging gleams. But he found none.

Ahead was a rockier channel. He prowled in the splashing water, past the glossy sweep over boulders and among the tufts of white foam from the lower sides of the stones. No quick little fins cut away from him. He was fooled once by the silver blades of air between floating blades of reeds. But the fish, like the frogs, all had vanished.

Even the clams were gone. Among tassels of algae ruffling off stones he often had found a tassel that crossed the stream. That, he had learned, was algae growing upon the shell of a clam. To stop motion so slow was not thrilling, but he had liked clam meat. The flavor was only a memory, almost forgotten now.

Up out of the stream, racing along the bank on a trail worn by moose and deer, the Mink did find a garter snake. The snakes, too, were becoming scarce, but he finally detected the slip of one under a stalk of Oregon grape. A pounce, a bite on its head, and the Mink stopped to lie on his haunches and elbows, eating the snake. When it was gone, he slept.

The cottonwood grove he had reached was the lowest point on his travel route. Here a small creek joined the stream, and always before he had turned back along it, up the valley floor again to the base of the Tetons and the pine forest where he preferred to range.

Daylight was leveling through the grove when he woke. The pines he had left behind were as full now as they had been through the summer, but here a brisk wind was tearing the leaves from the cottonwood boughs. The trunks were hoary with bare gray twigs; the stripped branches, massed above, seemed a cloudiness in the sky. Flowers had withered; leaves already fallen were dry and brittle. Even if all of his favorite food, the fish, frogs, snakes, and many more creatures had not disappeared, one might wake on this day with a feeling that the world had altered; and the Mink did not like changes. But the birds might be here! To catch them had been his chief game in this grove.

He blinked and stretched; then looked out more steadily. Soon he eased forward. Around him, of course, were mice. He caught a few, eating none, piling them under the side of a log. He bounded about on a hunt for the birds, and his stomping tread seemed like a frisking, but his eyes were not playful. His need had intensified. It showed in the reaching look of his face, in his motions' anguished impatience, and his poignant high cry when he leapt for a junco, and it flew away.

This morning no red-shafted flickers were standing alert on the anthills, tilting downward to snatch lively bites. No tail of a song sparrow twitched in the weeds. Now on the stream bank, the Mink watched the water. The ripples were rocking their chips of sky, but no spotted sandpipers bobbed on their long submerged legs, as if tipped by the current. What delight it had been to check neatly the varied movements of all those birds!

In his flat little skull was no space for the brain tissue that functions morally, for imagination that whispers: *the bird might prefer to live.* Instinct was all the guidance he had, and adjustment to it was his kind of integrity. He might have lived lazily — and enjoyed it, for vivid exertion may be no easier for an animal than it is for a man. But a different urge was the mainspring of his nature. He must constantly spend his energy, and for a purpose: to stop other animals' lives. That was it — find the motion of fish, mouse, frog, bird, or other creature and end it!

A few he would eat; more would be cached. The whole slaughter had a relation to keeping fed. He hid most of his victims in some pretense, at least, of a cranny, though it might be only the shade of a clod of mud. His motives, hunger and sport, were mixed, but he never killed coldly, never deliberately. Sometimes he captured only enough animals for that day. At other times he took more, because of his restless excitement, or a sense of extra need, as now with winter ahead.

On this day in September he did not return to the forest along the mountains. Instead he went out through the cottonwood grove to the sagebrush plain beyond. The flat was strange, not his kind of place, yet some new urge sent him toward it.

Under his feet was a pavement of pebbles and rocks carried down from the mountains and spread on the valley floor by old glaciers. Since colors were only varying shades of gray to the Mink, he could not see that stones of white quartz were mingled richly with pink and red feldspar, blue limestone, and black shale. But his nose may have done what a human nose could not: smelled differences in the stones, which were of different ages by millions of years. They did not, anyway, smell like the wet stones of river banks.

He found tracks and the burrows of animals, but none scented like those he knew. An elk had passed here, and here a coyote, a jack rabbit, a badger; and deer mice who smelled of the sage seeds they ate, not of angelica, reed-grass, and other plants of moist places.

This was country to cross, not explore. With his back a tensed bow, he bounded over the stones, winding between the sage clumps, heading east as directly as if he had covered this route many times. Now and then he would jump, trying to catch a nighthawk or thrasher, but they and their manners were unfamiliar, and he missed them all. A sweeping wind, unchecked by a single tree, blew sand in his eyes and fur. The strain in his small face became even tighter. He had almost the look of a creature pursued.

He came to a bench where the plain terraced down abruptly. There on the brink his heart could relax. For below was a marsh in the flood-plain of the Snake River. Sounds of the river's flow and wind entangled in trees, the odors of mushrooms, the mold on wet bark, the freshness of quick decay: these sensations were home to a mink more than any particular stream is. They greeted him here.

He descended the short bluff and came to a meadow of reed-grass, lush even in autumn. Finding a moose's trail in it, he bounded along to the river. He ran downstream among the willow shrubs on the bank, sniffing, peering among the roots, a weaving prance. He was exhilarated by some possibility, not yet clear.

Soon he went down to the water's edge. Out in the river a bar, a spine of rocks, humped up white through the current. Farther along, the bar joined the bank, thus enclosing a narrow slough. Just as winds throw their loads into corners on land, the river had pocketed dead leaves, grass, and twigs in it. The Mink, starting on to the bar, plunged out into the trash.

Sparks flared and streaked into sinuous silver lightning — fish! Little dace and trout, setting off one another's fear, sprayed away through the litter. The Mink tried to throw himself after a gleam, lost it. For the fish, flexible living darts, could dodge through the leaves in quick elongated quivers. But the tangle entrapped the Mink. Loose root fibers knotted around his feet. Masses of soaked reed-grass weighted his neck.

With a dive, a creeping, a few swimming strokes as he could, he crossed the slough, reaching the bar. He bounded along to its tip. Ahead was clear water, the swirl past the mouth of the slough to the swift-running channel.

A trout nearly as long as he, larger than any he'd seen, was passing, lacing its way upstream. Amazing, essential prey! He sprang into the water, put every trace of his strength in his tail-swing and the paddling push of his feet. But the river, too, was a mightiness yet undreamed of. The trout seemed to slice through its force without effort, but the Mink had to battle it.

He continued pursuing the motions ahead, but now they were only the current's white streaks of light. Finally he held his stroke, reeled around in the flow, and, letting the river carry him, guided his drift to the bar again.

At its high end was the stranded root-crown of a tree. The Mink lay beneath it, chin on his outspread forepaws and his eyes looking forth with unblinking intensity.

The only streams he had known were those he could span with a leap or two, currents in which a mink could catch any fish that he glimpsed. And fish had been plentiful until recently. For those high streams were the spawning grounds for adult trout and bullheads that lived in the lower rivers and lakes. The eggs hatched; the young fry became fingerlings. But the upper brooks would freeze solid in winter. Therefore instinct had given the small fish an impulse to go down to the open Snake. The Mink, though not knowing consciously where the fish were, had been following them.

He must find new ways to catch them here. He must discover where they were hiding and must strengthen his swimming to meet the force of the river. Everywhere were the signs of its conquering. Logs, trees torn from the land, were strewn at each bend. Shattered branches and willow skeletons lay on the bar. Wreckage was draped around every living willow upon the banks. If the river's throaty, incessant roar did not warn of its mastery, no eye could miss proofs of it.

The Mink listened and watched, not analyzing the unfamiliar problems but taking them into his senses for intuition to solve.

He was away from the root-crown, diving, streaking through the flow to the bank on the out-curve. Below it a bullhead, a sculpin, held its place with a rippling of fins. At sight of the Mink the bullhead darted along the bank. But the Mink swerved, overtook it, clamped his jaws on its neck, and killed it. With the fish in his mouth he struggled back through the water's swift pressure. And now, as he ran up the bar, he was flinging his head, switching the fish about, triumphant as he had not been with the captured mice.

Again under the root-crown, he lay with his fish in his paws. His sharp little ivory teeth pierced through the bullhead's skin to the pearly flesh and the skull, which broke as thin ice does, with a crackle. In a fair chase he had caught the fish. The quick precision with which his dive spiraled was one of nature's perfections. And now he ate every shred of the prey, every bone and fin. Fish at last! . . . flesh that his own flesh especially demanded.

In the soak of leaves over the slough, a skid of light! The Mink leapt. And this time he caught a dace. Running back to the root-crown, he left it; then sped to the slough again, for his eyes held an after-image of gleams fanning out as he pounced. A new possibility tripped his nerves. If he himself jumped toward the water beyond the slough, could he drive out the dace and trout?

He could! He forced them away from the trash. A whole

school of the bright little fish fled up along the bank. His teeth snapped on one of the slivers of life. He dropped it beside a shoreline rock, flashed again to the water, caught a second fish, left it, chased the rest, caught more, more, and more until every one had been stopped.

Sped by exhilaration, he ran on up the river. Often he dived in the water, eager to think any movement a fish. Finding that he was mistaken, he would swim a short way but return soon to the bank, where he could feel himself race along without opposition from any current, not now caring that he might be seen there as easily as if he had been a brown stain flowing over the pebbles, milky-white with dried mud.

The fish were only a first discovery. The Mink arrived soon at a wilderness drama as instructive as if it had happened in order to show him in one quick lesson where to find winter food.

As he followed the river, he came to an inflowing creek. The creek was running at full flood. Any stream in spate is exciting, in the way that it captures land things, trees, brush, and sod, nests of birds, mice, and shrews, and often the occupants. The torrent seems a non-living predator.

The Mink would see many such floods in the spring, when the valley waterways would be draining off snow deep enough to have buried a moose. But Cottonwood Creek at flood stage in September had the feel of disaster, like an avalanche or a lightning-set fire. His curiosity flared.

He found the cause. Through a break in a beaver dam the marsh he had seen was pouring down into the creek. The outer canals of the marsh were empty, the main pond had dropped, and the animals had sensed an emergency. He came to the shore through a stand of sedges. His nose parted the blades, and he saw the whole scene, devastation for the community but supreme luck for him.

The small bay here is alive with a little brown horde, trying to stay with their watery home as it ebbs away. The Mink, out on the mud, makes a quick savage bite of a dragonfly nymph, a scud, ram's-horn and physa snails, caddisworms. One caddisworm dragged a shelter he'd made by cementing together tiny living snails. The Mink's teeth crushed the whole thing, unwilling guests and their host. And more and more dragonfly nymphs — they were the meaty prey. He had enjoyed them all summer, but recently they had disappeared.

Get the salamander, stop the soft lizardlike body coiling into the willow roots! The Mink pawed it out, coming on several others. They had formed a winter colony with unusual speed today, but the Mink broke it up. He punctured their necks and cast them aside on the mud.

The bay was bewildering with its odors of frogs, fish, snakes, water insects, and other creatures, and with its quivers and flicks of movement. As the Mink stood on the shiny silt, his shoulders and head swayed above his forelegs. To leap at the small stranded bullhead flapping there, or the yellow warbler alighting to snatch a skater, or the leech, or the shrew?

A Varying Hare! Between willows on shore passed a stream of white, and the Mink caught a rabbitlike scent that recalled a delicious victim his mother had brought once to the den. He was away in pursuit of the Hare.

Her motion was fluff. Leading into the water-meadow, she bounded ahead like a ball of white cloud, touching the earth with a round lightness, rocking along, it seemed with no strain whatsoever. A mink should catch that! Sharp and dark he pierced after her, eyes and nose streaming along her white scent.

He lost sight of her in the grass but was close enough so that he stayed in her trough, parting the stems himself before they had quieted after her bounding. There again was the gleam of her heels, tossing back airy leaps. She had crossed the meadow, was circling the backwash of the beaver pond, under aspens. She was clearly in sight. Amazing, that he had not reached her! He drove himself even faster. The Hare topped the bank beyond with a single leap. And the Mink, with his much shorter jumps, fell so far behind that he had to give up the chase. The defeat was maddening, especially now in the midst of so much success.

He whipped about through the grove on the west shore of the pond, at first merely expressing the anger that lashed him but little by little becoming interested in any crevice suggesting a place to rest. A mink-sized cave under the bank of the Beaver's canal would be fair protection, but he searched farther. This hollow space under the edge of a loose piece of sod? This cranny between two boulders? He found muskrat scent, old to be sure, in the debris at the base of a fir tree, scraped the trash away, and discovered the upper exit to a den. He ran down the burrow to the nest hole, abandoned and exactly large enough for a mink. He followed the light trickling in through the entrance burrow and came to a second opening in the bank of the pond. The dim odor of muskrat filled him with yearning, but the den, even without the owner, was gratifying. He lay in the entrance for a while, almost wanting to sleep; then set out again, leaving the burrow with feelings of ownership.

He swung about on the soppy silt of the lowered shores,

where each of his footprints became a miniature puddle. There ahead was a really large puddle, and in it were several land-locked suckers! Ordinarily they were dull fish but now were excited, for they sensed that they were cut off from the pond.

The Mink saw them and was frantic to catch them, but he did not dare to approach the pool, for an Otter was standing beside it. He never had seen an otter before. It looked like a giant mink with a sharper-keeled tail, with eyes as intense as a mink's but more open, seeking but not belligerent. A mink that size surely could have any prey that he wanted. Yet the Otter was watching the suckers and making no effort to take them.

The Mink swung back and forth, staying up near the bank but gradually working out farther. The Otter had seen him but made no move either of interest or aggression. The Mink risked a little sinuous sally, close to the edge of the puddle. Still the Otter ignored him. With a very bold darting, then, the Mink leapt in the pool, snatched a sucker, and raced away with it.

He cached it under willow roots and again cautiously, but more quickly this time, tacked to the puddle. Would the big Otter actually allow him to take another fish? It seemed that he would; he was turning away — satiated? Or knowing a better supply of perhaps tastier fish? The suckers would please the Mink. He caught every one and left them together, a pile of food that no doubt gave him a sense of security as well as a sense of conquering.

He continued to prowl, to stop a creeping, a gliding, a flut-tering when he could. But many animals had found hideaways, and the Mink himself was becoming tired. Even yet, though, he was not willing to return to his new shelter, not when every step took him across a fresh scent.

The end of the backwash was banked with rocks. The Mink

saw the hind foot of a frog pull in under one of the cobbles. He dug out the frog, took a bite of it, hunted beneath more and more of the stones, and found other frogs. He severed their heads and abandoned them. On the west side of the backwash his eye glimpsed a garter snake, sliding into a cobbled crevice. But he could not have the snake. The surrounding rocks were so tightly packed in dry earth that he could not claw them away.

His sight of the frogs and snake had made some disconnected parts of his intuition swing together. Without telling himself where these creatures would spend the winter, he would begin now to turn over stones.

Today too he had seen a migration of water insects and snails toward the center of the pond. He would find them there, in the unfrozen depths, until spring. In the river and here at the marsh were the visible answers to the question that his nerves had been asking: where was his summer food? His eyes had seen various prey creatures enter their cold-weather quarters, and his nerves would remind him.

The Mink was fed, but his day had had one great disappointment — he had not caught the Hare. As he turned toward the muskrat den, he again saw her, sitting behind a stand of white daisies.

He pursued her once more, through berry bushes, thistles, and aspen brush. But suddenly, as if tufts of her softness were flying, snow surrounded him. The snow, falling in huge downy flakes, did not seem to begin; without any advance flurries it was coming down, filling the air. The Mink never had seen snow before. He was confused and lost the white puff bounding over the ground ahead of him.

Retracing his way to the den, he stepped out on the bank.

There below, crouched at the muddy shore, was a young merganser. The Mink dived through the snow so swiftly that she had time to make only one quick, spasmodic flutter as his jaws snapped on her throat.

Her flesh, tasting fishy because the merganser had lived on fish, was new to the Mink and sharply pleasing to him. And so he had one more meal, although he had eaten too much already and would not have been tempted by any food except this, which combined the flavors of fish and bird. But he had to leave half the catch. Walking slowly and heavily, with his slim little belly extended until it was almost as round as the Hare's, he returned to the den, crept to the nest cavity, curled up there in the darkness, and fell at once into a long blank sleep.

Back in the pine forest where the Mink had begun his migration, a colony of tired deer mice and meadow mice also were sleeping, fitted into their miniature dens and their nest balls of shredded grass. They were exhausted, for a mighty battle had taken place in their range. Early that morning they had discovered a cache of seven dead mice at the base of a stump.

The flesh of their own kind was acceptable to them, was indeed a great treat to them, although they did not often attack one another. A feast of seven, fresh and nourishing, had been especially important at this time, because the storm's approach made their hunger too great to be satisfied seed by seed. They had fought for the unexpected food, and a few of the sleepers were wounded, but none had been killed. All were luxuriously fed. Fate, on this crucial day, had been good to them.

On a bar in the Snake River three gulls stood parallel in the lee of a stranded log. For two days, as the weather threatened, they had searched for a meal of abandoned fish. But few of the predators were leaving half-eaten carcasses at this time, when all appetites were particularly keen. The gulls were in danger of having to wait out the snow with their energy weakened. But late in the morning fortune had awarded them a fine meal. One had sighted a Mink, streaming along the white rocks of the river bank. Following back on his course, the gulls had come to a line of young trout and dace, left at the edge of the water. In a brief tumult of cries and tossed wings, the gulls had divided the hoard.

A diverse crowd of small scavengers took their last bites from a scattering of dead salamanders, strewn about in a drained bay of the marsh. At the end of the backwash a snake had come out of his winter den, drawn by the odor of slain frogs on the mud below. But he hadn't been able to reach them, because a flock of ravens discovered the carnage, too, and scrambled among themselves for the chance thus to fortify their great, handsome, black bodies. A kingfisher was pleased to have been the only one to find a cache of mountain suckers beneath a willow. He already had eaten two.

On the other side of the pond a muskrat had emerged timidly from the Beaver's lodge, where she lived. She was hungry, for she had been afraid to come out since the fall of the pond had exposed the house entrance. But dusk gave her courage. And she didn't have to go far for a meal. At the foot of the bank, nearly concealed in the snow, was a partially eaten merganser. The muskrat had neither the wit nor the speed to catch a live duck, but she found that she liked the taste of the meat. The white crystals clung to her fur and to the bird's feathers, so that soon all was white. It seemed but the merest rumpling of down when the muskrat took a new bite or shifted her hold.

Finally all the bounties were consumed. The last clean bones were discarded, and the well-fed animals turned to their shelters and sleep.

The Mink had not stirred. His den was snug and comfortable, with the warmth of the earth held in, as it was, by the snow. For many of the plants the snow's gentle touch was death. It continued to fall, a soft new cover for every flake.

The Varying Hare

☼

The dry shine of the moon, that night, showed that the leaves were breaking away from the boughs. They were taking flight — like the small birds who had perched among them, were off in the air, free and wild. During previous weeks a few had drifted out singly, but, released by the wind, they departed in flocks.

As the Varying Hare hopped along her paths, leaves would race by above her. Others would skitter ahead on the ground, to drop when the wind slackened and then, caught up by the next gust, whirl away through the impatient rooted grasses.

When the sun rose in the morning, the Hare was back in her form. It was a fragile home, only a space between willow shrubs, but it always had been a pocket of shadow, where she was concealed on the brightest day. Now, however, she tried to hide among streaming lights. The blowy night had torn holes in her overhead screen, and the sun found its way through them.

The wind had died before dawn, for it was veering. But a fresh breeze was swinging the willows and swinging farther and faster the scraps of sunshine below. The branches would strain to one side, with a look of agonized tension would quiver against the wind's drive, and a new little covey of leaves would escape. Then the gust would withdraw its pressure. The riven boughs would spring back, and the beams, wider now, would flow over the Hare.

To keep herself smooth, she sat facing the wind. Ahead were more willows, pierced for the first time by the glare of the pond. Her eyes, at the sides of her head, could see also the water-meadow behind her. The reed-grass there had stood tall and thick until recently, but, in dying, had bent down in hillocks. On the west side of the meadow, along the backwash of the pond, aspen brush grew on a low ridge of drier ground. It was thinner this morning. In the glittering tops was the shape of the boughs' coming bareness.

The Hare had been crouching with feet beneath her and ears flat along her neck. It was her sleeping position, as smooth as a weather-worn mound of earth. But this day she could not relax. She sat back like a small bundle suddenly breaking open. First licking the dust from the hairy palms of her forepaws, she scrubbed her face 'round and 'round, rolling her head. With her paws she pulled one of her long ears down against her cheek and brushed it; and brushed her other ear, and her sides, and back; and washed her hind feet. To be clean seemed to smooth her emotions, too. She lowered her ears, pulled in her head, and nestled into her form, the depression matching her shape, that her weight had hollowed. Openings in the branches above might expose her, but nothing had changed the cozy sensation beneath her, and she would console herself with it.

Even after she closed her eyes, she could feel the new, unfamiliar lights darting over them. Soon, though, no more of them touched her lids. She looked up and imperceptibly started, shrinking lower. For a marsh hawk was hovering over her thicket.

The feathered cross, balancing on the wind, broke the gleams in the leaves with a shadow, one shadow she did not like. It hung in the air, swaying, sliding off as the hawk let the wind push him back but swinging forward again, tilting and leveling down, a threat that waited, a silent torment that still did not strike, never quite motionless but patient with the sense of its power.

The Hare was shaken with terror. She cast a frantic glance toward the reed-grass and under adjoining willows; there was no deeper gloom in which she could hide. The hawk could not drop through the branches, even if they were entirely bare, but the Hare was excitable, likely to flee in a panic. Again he rode back on the wind, for an instant was blurred by the churning of blown boughs, but he swept ahead, dropping lower, and opened his claws and beak.

The Hare's fear was now at the last bearable point of its tension. Yet she did not break. The hope of the hawk already was sagging when his eye caught a quiver of grass at the side of her thicket. He turned, dipped, and alighted, his claw clutching a mouse.

He stayed on the ground while he ate it, near the Hare but not able to reach her and not once shifting his angry eyes in her direction. When he had finished his small meal, he lifted his wings and soared up and away.

The Hare continued to crouch in her form, with no sign to reveal the decision her nerves were making. Through half the summer these willows had been her refuge. She had been born on the other side of the meadow, under the aspen brush, but one day, returning there after a little canter, she had found a very disturbing thing. It was her mother's foot, with the scent of mink all around it. She had left the aspens then, to stay under these willows. She still kept the aspens for one of her covert-nooks, into which she could dodge when she was in danger, but the willows had been her form — till this morning. She no longer could trust them, now that a hawk had threatened her through their broken screen. Whether or not she knew it yet, she had lost the sense that this hideaway was her home.

Beside the fall of the leaves, the Hare had another problem — she herself had begun to shine. Several weeks before, her brown fur had started to shed when she licked it. Beneath, growing up through her undercoat, was a new kind of hairs, white, the color to her of the noonday sun.

First her feet had turned white, and the fur on her soles had become long and stiff. When she bounded over the ground, spreading her toes, she came down on thick, springy pads and left much wider footprints. Denser white fur had grown over her ears. In summer the near-naked skin of her ears had helped her lose warmth and be comfortable. A few frosty nights had proved that they soon would need coverings. Her legs, then hips, shoulders, chest, and sides had whitened. On this day of the equinox only parts of her face and a strip down her back still were brown.

From her earliest life the Hare's eyes had led her away from the revealing sunlight. And now she could not escape any-where from her own glisten. She was luminous even, because bubbles of air in her new hairs caught every faint gleam and en-closed her in a halo. Nature, having taught her to hide, had made hiding impossible.

Her instinct was groping for some solution.

Leave the thicket here, it suggested. A push on her toes sent her up in a rounded hop. Her forepaws touched earth, one then the other, to ease her down. Her hind feet, leap-frogging over, dropped in front of them . . . springing at once in a second soft bound. She didn't stretch out at full length when she jumped; she held her legs close to her, so that she tumbled ahead like a curl of white swan's-down, blowing.

She was passing the meadow, on a path she had flattened between the reed-grass and the shoreline willows. A few times she dodged into the brush, into her own familiar covert-nooks. On all of her trails she had shelters, with clear openings under the boughs that she could enter without a pause. She knew the location of each, the angle at which to approach it, and the pattern of leaps — alighting here, here, and here — that would take her to safety most quickly. This morning the shadows in all the nooks were as shredded as in her form, and she didn't stay long in any.

Rounding the Leopard Frog's puddle, then, she came to the aspen brush. A small, slow, conclusive hop took her under, and she huddled down in soft earth. The branches above her were nearly stripped, and the sun, splashing into the shelter here, may have shocked her more than the light in the willows did. For this nook was the kindling place where she and her brother and sister had come into life. More precocious than little rabbits, the hares were born fully furred and with open eyes. Soon they had been able to swing their ears to their mother's delicate bounds approaching, and to the terrible screams of ravens, harsh as rocks breaking on rocks. Their mother had left at once and returned only to feed her leverets. It was the aspen leaves that protected them from the menacing birds above, from hawks, owls, and eagles, as well as the ravens.

The leaves' silken incessant whisper had been as comforting to the Hare as the touch of her mother's tongue, licking her while she nursed. And ever since, there had been a happy relationship between the Hare, who avoided light, and the leaves, which layered themselves into a cover in order to find it. Leaves had another meaning. She had been only a week old when she crept out, with motions as unaggressive as theirs, tasted a stalk of sorrel, and found its sharp flavor as good in her mouth as milk. Her life had been filled with the ministrations of leaves. They were the lovable things to the Hare, as stones were to the marmots and logs to the salamanders.

And now suddenly they were deserting her. They were failing her neighbors too, that fall morning. The grass near the aspen brush glinted with dragonfly wings. Every summer evening the dragons had gathered, for some reason they knew, at this small part of the meadow. Clinging low on the stems, they were sheltered from wind and cold as they slept. Moose had rested here in the sunshine, but the grass always rose again when they left — until one day late in August. When the insects came home that night, they found that their grass was flat. Some had sought other perches, but many had settled onto the prostrate blades and, exposed there, had frozen. Water-shrews had eaten their bodies and discarded the wings.

On the other side of the Hare the movements of mourning doves smoothed past her gaze. The birds walked about in the bed of sorrel, selecting a seed from a stalk here and farther along another. Their heads tilted gently to examine the seeds and then nodded with each intimately touching step. The foraging was sedate and slow, although the birds must have sensed that the marsh plants, which had fed them with buds, seeds, and berries, soon would have nothing more for them.

Beyond the doves was the pond. Thirsty, the Hare left her nook and set herself down in several airy jumps to the shore. As she lapped the water, a muskrat passed, swimming home with a sheaf of cut bur-reeds in her mouth. All the floating reeds had been ice-coated this morning. Farther along the shore a pintail stood in a mat of the plants that human beings named bedstraw, because they liked to believe that the Christ child's manger was filled with something so tiny and sweet. The duck was tweaking off ends of the sprays, where seeds had replaced the little white flowers. The duck, the doves, muskrat, the Hare, and most other plant-eating creatures were a company of the harmless — almost too mild and shy, it seemed, to meet such a violent change as the coming of winter.

The Hare, having drunk, was ready herself for food. She nipped a clover stem close to the root and drew it in, bite by bite, as she chewed. Then she reached for another, forepaws hopping ahead and hind feet stepping up leisurely to enclose them. The leaves of the clover were smaller now than in summer, and she didn't find one blossom with its delectable honey taste. Whole parts of the patch were bare, for she had cropped it through many weeks, and the clover was only attempting to stay alive; it no longer was growing. As she munched along, her eyes were half-closed with dreamy pleasure, but her ears were alert, lightly turning in separate directions or swinging in unison. They were sensitive ears; when all the green plants of the marsh were expanding, they may have caught a minute murmur of growth. If they reached now for that sound, they found only silence.

The Hare came to a gentian, a marsh bluebell, and a lupine — all fresh, as if the season, for them alone, were spring. They were but three small flowers; when she severed a stalk of meadowsweet, the dust of its dead blooms fell over her. Her bite, jarring a silky white head of goldenrod, loosened it, and it blew away. She ate and enjoyed the fine blades of blue-grass, although they were dry; but she found that a fireweed had a coarser harsh flavor. Most of the plants had a different taste now, bitter, as if they resented what the autumn was doing to them.

The Hare turned back to the aspen nook but as soon as her meal was digested wanted to leave. No other place lured her; she had merely a sense that sitting under these boughs was no longer the thing to do. She hopped along one of her paths in the meadow, reached a moose-bed, and found herself leaping straight up and down! She was making showy white bounds higher, even, than the heads of the standing grasses! The next time she sprang in the air, she twisted herself at the top of the leap so that she came to earth faced the opposite way. She jumped again, turned about, and reversed her direction. She had done this before. It was a comic impulse that slipped through her caution occasionally, but always till now in the dark of night. And here she was hurling her dazzling new self into sunlight!

Bounding across the meadow, she came to a line of willow shrubs. She had covert-nooks here but didn't go into them. She leapt, instead, over a thicket — a great arc that brought her down on the other side, in a place new to her.

This was a flat ledge behind the bank of a river, which the Hare had avoided because she would be too exposed on its low bed of scouring rushes and moss. Now, however, she raced about over it as if she were chasing some invisible playmate. At the edge of the water she stopped, resting upon her haunches, with her forelegs straightened below her shoulders. The river's swift movement, its rush and roar seemed to excite her. She swung back, sitting upright, and whirled her forepaws in the air.

But other hares should be here. Her heart may have felt suddenly pinched by the strangeness, for she turned away from the heavy tide, rolling past, and thumped on the ground with one of her hind feet. It was a hare's way of signaling to companions, and after she pounded a few times, she would listen. No one answered. She left the river, passed the willows, and was once more in her meadow. She would return to the aspens, for uneasiness swept her.

As she was bounding along her trail, the marsh hawk swung over the aspen tops. Even before he had cleared them, the Hare's eyes had detected his smooth streaming behind the last quivering leaves. How long her hops now — and how swift! She was leaping at mad speed, sure of the entrance among the boughs. But the hawk was crossing the aspens, was swooping down, and had leveled above her with spread claws toward her back.

Into the narrowing instant dived an enemy of the hawk himself. A young Osprey, seeing a chance to torment his foe, struck out from his perch. The wings of the birds entangled, the two beat their way off toward the lower end of the pond.

The Hare was safe under her brush, forgotten if not concealed.

Her heart's thumping rocked her, but not for long. At the edge of the pond the Leopard Frog thrashed about in a heron's beak. The Hare watched them, so interested that her fears began slipping away. A bull Moose and a cow raced out over the meadow. The hoofs' pounding startled the Hare, but she turned, in order to see the huge creatures clearly, and soon was curious more than alarmed. In their chase was a weird buffoonery, like a great grotesque shadow of her own antic racing.

Something in her temperament seemed to be opening out, since she was white and almost everywhere sun-lighted, and no longer could hide. The loosening of her secretiveness had been paced with the changes of autumn. It was slow at first, now was progressing more rapidly. Inasmuch as the leaves were falling, exposing hideaways, all the animals were compelled to face each other as they had not in the summer. Others besides the Hare were darting about with new courage, or a new reliance on bluff.

She started forth again. While she was sitting among the sedges, eating a tuber, a furious gust of wind blew over the dead tree where the Osprey had perched. Even the snags and the bare boughs, as well as the grass and leaves, seemed to be coming down.

The crash of the tree frightened her, as it did all the animals, but she soon recovered her poise and went about, savoring her new sense of freedom. The tree had been part of the beaver dam, and its overturn opened the dam, letting the pond start to flow away. The lowering of the water made the Hare's neighbors, those who lived in the pond or entered it, apprehensive. Some already were suffocating in the dry air that their gills could not breathe. Surrounded by panic, the Hare jumped and tumbled in droll solitary games. She had not played as much at any time since her brother and sister left to find homes somewhere outside the marsh.

Had her new boldness, though, come too soon? She was racing around through the willow brush when the wind, blowing up from the shore, brought an acrid scent — Mink!

Her next hop was twice as long — but the Mink had discovered her. Half-giddy with fear, she led away toward the meadow. While her eyes found the path ahead, she could see backward, too, see the dark pointed face penetrating the grasses behind her. The Mink held his spine in a high rigid arch, putting all his energy into the throw of his legs. They were short; he must make many more leaps than she did. She could outrun him, but his tenacity was the terror. Where could she go that he could not trail her? Where could she lose that nose, seeking along her scent? He was quick, sharp, and sure. His vitality was electric. And in her was the wide reluctance of a peaceable creature, now frantic . . . and with numbness . . . beginning to blur in her head.

Her dizziness was a symptom of shock. She was susceptible to it. Varying hares often died when no predator's tooth touched them. Or they might collapse if they did not die. Then, unable to move, they would seem to give up to the hunter. This Hare's race was as much against fright as the Mink.

Her path reached the isthmus between the backwash and the river. It bent there abruptly along the west side of the aspens. She would have followed it back, but the Mink, sensing the likely turns in a hare's trail, took a shortcut and blocked her.

She flung herself on. The only way open was the bank at the end of the isthmus. With one leap she had mounted it. Bounding along its top, she came to a brook, jumped it, and entered the grove of tall trees she had seen from across the pond.

This was out of her range, a place where she never had come before. Desperate, confused, yet she made a hare's canny circular trail. She crossed a small clearing, from its other side wound around through the grove to the shore again. There, finding some thimbleberry stalks, she stopped under their big drooping leaves and looked out toward the course she had taken.

The Mink appeared, as she expected. Guided by only her scent now, he bounded more slowly. Where she had leapt a log, he must stop to sniff. She saw his slim-bodied prowl, side to side, as he searched; and smelled the musk of his rage. But did he not, after all, have the patience to trail her? He snapped up a cricket, growled his anger, and turned away from her track.

The Hare, exhausted, sagged into a flatter mound. A slanting shadow, that of a raven, crossed a cottonwood trunk. She paid no attention to it, nor to the new kinds of food here.

The wind had passed. Even the tiny straw flowers of bluegrass hung motionless on their hairlike threads. Birds were silent. The brook tinkled, and the pond poured away through the gap. But all living things were still. The earth darkened — a change that pleased the Hare. Cloudiness to her was not in the sky; it was a shade on the ground, gloom like this in which everywhere she felt hidden. She relaxed and slipped into a thin little sleep.

The earth and the Hare waited, for what? . . . not a thunderclap. Few Jackson Hole creatures had heard autumn rain, dripping on dead leaves or spattering in blown gusts. By the time that the leaves were down, winter was ready to strike.

A quick wind made the Hare shiver. It seemed to rise from the ground, for the treetops were quiet. The flowers and grasses jerkily stirred. All the moist odors sharpened.

The scent again of the Mink! The Hare saw his eyes, reared to look over the white heads of daisies. She was facing him, but she sprang in the air, whirled about, and came to earth ready to bound in the other direction.

She sped back in the grove. The Mink was pursuing her. Here she could not flee with the sureness she could on familiar trails. She began to dodge, in a wild darting, to bewilder him. But his eyes hardly could lose her, puff of white, lifting over the grasses, the flowers, the thickets. She did not lose him, either. The deep-shaded ground helped to hide his dark fur, but the naked light soles of his feet still flashed there behind, as he bounded.

Once more she felt dizzy. Then, with a soft suddenness, a white confusion enveloped her. Between her and the Mink a white mist was descending. At the start of a leap it would screen off her landing place. She must jump blindly, and she no longer could see the Mink.

Finally she dared to pause. He did not appear. She continued to wait. But no angular leaps broke the blurring around her. She was sitting upright, half-turned to listen and watch, while over her gently, silently, dropped the snow. It was a new kind of cover, enfolding her with a lightness exactly matching her coat. It glistened as she did; even its motion was airy and mild, like hers. Lovely it came, more delicate than the finest leaves. Its fall was the happening that her heart and nerves had been waiting for.

The snow was heaping over the rocks, plants, and clods of

earth, strewing the woodland with mounds that were hare-sized and hare-shaped. With a bound she put herself on a log. Already she sensed that a world smooth and white like herself called for a different kind of caution — not to hide, to be up on a lookout. She drew herself into her roundest shape, with eyes open, keeping all the horizon in view. Now none of her dark-furred enemies could slip up, undetected. And when she wanted to rest she could make a form in the snow. Her ears were pressed deep in the fur on her neck, but were outward-turned, and were hearing a strange tiny swish.

The air cleared before dusk. Down through the white-cushioned boughs the sun spread a glow. It was gone quickly. Even after it faded, the light seemed to be held in this pale grove. But a new mist of flakes started falling, and night crept in through the trees.

The Hare was hungry. She took a bite of the snow. It became a drink in her mouth. She took others. Then she bounded away from her log, out onto the earth's curious cover. She was not surprised that it held her up, but its surface was downy. Even her thickly furred snowshoe-feet sank a little way into it. Though it did not give her the solid resistance the ground did, she learned quickly to push with a lighter touch. She found herself going faster than she could when she threaded the brush and grasses.

What should she eat? All the low plants were buried. The shrubs had huge blossoms of snow, but she was not deceived by them. Instinct directed her to the brook she had leapt when she entered the grove. Aspens and willows lined it. She stretched up from her hind toes, snipped off twigs and buds, and ate them, finding new flavors. She even enjoyed the puckery bark of the larger boughs. Thickets like these, familiar as shelters, would stand higher than even the deepest snows and furnish her winter food.

Turning back to the grove, she stopped at a fir tree for a tuft of the needles that grew from the trunk. She would have liked more of them, but moose had browsed off the firs, so that the trunks held aloft spindles of only their topmost branches. Spruce boughs were hanging in low, sweeping sprays, so close to the snow that the Hare could reach up to them. She sniffed at the needle-wrapped twigs, but found that the spruce flavor tempted her no more than it did the moose.

She bounded along the shore of the pond, passed the beaver house, and went on to the end of the dam, where it joined the bank. There she found a fine lookout, up on a stump, and cuddled into the white puff that capped it.

The pond was low, most of it having drained away. But the Beaver was working, filling the break in the dam with cut boughs. He made endless trips to the willow thickets; would return, dragging his timbers, fit them in place, plaster them there, and go back for more. If he should not mend the dam, this community would become again what it once was: only the rocky flood-plain of the river. All the inter-dependent plants and animals would disperse; many would die, and even the Hare would have to find a home in some other wet leafy place. But the marsh was originally the work of the Beaver's family, and he had begun to restore it.

Soon after midnight the clouds blew away from under the moon. A powder of sparkles appeared on the snow. But the moon swung back over the grove; then the shade of the trees moved out onto the bank, onto the pond, reached the gap in the dam, and finally darkened the opposite shore. Still the Beaver continued his labor, and the Hare watched him.

One of the trumpeter swans had spent the night on the narrowed expanse of the black water. Most other creatures were sleeping. Every turn of the wind, however, brought to the Hare's nose the scent of the Moose. She knew where he was: standing among the trees, a towering bulk, so motionless that he seemed surly. But he did not alarm her. She understood that he did not eat hares, though she always avoided a moose's mightily thumping hoofs.

The bull blocked the Beaver's runway back into the woodland. Perhaps that was the reason the Beaver was using willows; he may have hesitated to pass the Moose. Toward the end of the night, however, he needed an aspen, so he climbed on shore and started to cut down the nearest tree. It fell with its top hanging over the pond. The bull stirred himself then. He wanted the leaves of the aspen, and let himself down the bank, and began stripping them.

The Beaver pulled at the aspen, to drag it away. And what happened next? The Hare did not wait to see. She knew only that the Moose was attacking the Beaver, that he reared and stomped and the Beaver fled into his house. The hoofs pounded the roof. Now the Moose was not comical. His rage seemed as wildly disastrous as the wind that uprooted the tree. It could wreck the marsh just as surely if he should destroy the Beaver.

With a long leap from her stump, the Hare was away in the grove, bounding off through the trees, so far that she no longer heard the blows. Still she went on, frightened, but also enjoying the sense of being up on a higher, wider earth, out in the open yet feeling sure that she didn't show. The moon found its way through the branches, to gleam starkly white on a small place here, and here on another. The Hare avoided the brightness at first. Soon she was crossing it.

Ahead was the brook and the clearing enclosed by it. Would she dare to go out on that meadow? She came to the edge of the trees and stopped there — for beyond was a racing, romping company of white varying hares.

Some were jumping straight up and down, springing high from their hind feet while their forepaws beat the air. Others were running under the leaps, to whirl back abruptly and begin jumping, themselves. Two were facing each other, hopping into the air and changing places with every leap. All the motions were droll and fast.

The games were silent; the keenest hunter could not have heard any sound. But one hare kept watch. At the side of the clearing he stood tall and alert, sniffing, peering about for the eye-shine of a predator, whose footfall, too, would be quiet to-night. His ears whirled at each snap of a frosted log and plop of snow discarded by weighted branches. One of the other hares came and reared up beside him. The first guard dropped onto all feet, and the second assumed his watch.

The young Hare wanted to join the others but was shy. She made a short run into the clearing and circled back under her tree. While she waited for more daring, the guard beat with his hind foot — a warning! Instantly all were gone.

The Moose ran across the meadow, with snorting breath and feet gashing into the snow. Beyond he plunged over the brook. Soon the pound of his vanishing hoofs was snow-muffled.

Where had the new playmates gone? Back to their ranges? The Hare hopped out into the moonlight alone. She flung herself into a tumbling leap, and another, meanwhile watching her shadow stretch long and snap back. She jumped — and this time one of the hares, who had returned, ran beneath her. Soon all the others were there and playing again. They were like merry little white ghosts, having a frolic, as hares often do. Their joy had been sprung by their new safety, the gift of the snow.

The American
Merganser

✺

On the shore, behind bur-reeds that swayed their cool stalks across the pond's glare, lay a gray duck, the Merganser. She was not resting. Her intense yellow eyes had the look of a bird in flight, and her auburn crest, streaming backward like hair, was full-spread with emotion. She was hiding — from a horde of demanding young, her own and another duck's. And she was hungry; but if she went out to fish, they would find her and torment her until she had fed them.

The sun had begun to drape long shadows down from the trees on the mountain slope. Now its light slanted under the wild-rose thicket that covered the duck. She opened a black and white wing so that the warmth would fall on her soft, new flight feathers. Any aid to their growing would bring nearer the time when the wing would be useful again, and she could escape from the marsh.

It was the season for flight — and the day. Water was blowing and breaking, was sucking and slapping among the spatterdock leaves with sounds restless and urgent. The sun had transferred the swing of the waves to the whole sheer face of the grove on the opposite shore. Over the white and gray bark, the leaves, and the green sprays of the spruces and firs sped a ravenous light, ghost of fire.

The very colors, this autumn day, would rouse all of a creature's wildness if he could see them, as the Merganser could. The red leaves of the rose thicket glowed with the sun behind them. Most of the fall flowers were blue — the marsh bluebells, gentians, aspen daisies, and lupines — but wine had splashed the bronze leaves of the Oregon grape, and the blowing aspens across the backwash were copper and yellow, a delicate dazzle above the combed sunlight on the brook. Over the trees, over the snows and the vertical pink rocks of the mountains, the sky was blue-black, dark because the air, without haze or dust, was so clear that one looked through it into the stratosphere's endless night. There was stillness . . . but clouds blew across it, ragged and shining like snow-banners torn from the Teton peaks.

The Merganser closed the warmed wing and turned and opened the other. The breeze tossed her crest up above her head, but she herself stayed as quiet as one of the cobblestones, nested here in the grass. Other birds were flying. During the afternoon the whole duck population had moved, the flocks, one after another, flaring up to alight in new bays or channels, no better but different. On a willow bough near the backwash a kingfisher twitched about, peering for fish. He complained in a voice like a magnified cricket's clatter and flung himself off, to seek the fish over the pond. A scarlet cap flashed on the white trunk of an aspen, as a downy woodpecker drilled for a wood-borer. He uncovered the slug, licked it out, rolled it back and forth on his tongue a few times, gulped it, and pitched off the tree to swing away through the grove. Two swallows flew up from the shore, tumbled easily skyward, side-slipped, rose, and met with a wing-touch.

A great blue heron stood motionless in the shallows beyond the reeds. He was holding his scrawny grace, intending the fish to forget he could move. The breeze swung the grasses, even jerked the dead snags; the heron looked less alive. But finally the bent tube of his neck straightened forward. His wings scooped up, and his lank feet trailed out of the water, as loosely he flapped off to alight in the sedge beds.

Even the heron flew. These birds too were molting, or recently had been, but their quills had dropped singly; there was never a time when the heron, the swallows, woodpecker, or kingfisher could not fly. The other ducks had been grounded as the Merganser was, since their wing feathers also came out all at once; but the rest of them had been back in the air for several weeks. The young mergansers were not flying because they were not yet that far developed. They and their mother were the only ducks still not able to tip themselves into the buoyant wind, feel it take them, support them while they streamed away, free.

To the young that experience was only a groping urge. The Merganser remembered it — how she would level out, with her low-hung throat and her long head pointing forward, and her feet pressed beneath her tail. As straight, herself, as the top of a pond, she would sweep ahead with unbroken speed.

If she could not fly on this fresh brilliant day, she could swim. She folded her wing to go into the pond — but still she must hold her impatience. A raven had started to jeer at her, and she would not appear to flee.

He had been soaring past, but saw her and stopped on a cottonwood branch. He worked so hard to annoy the duck that he flattened down on his perch and partly lifted his wings with each cry. The squawks seemed a lifeless clatter, which dropped at the end to a definite note as of something being closed upon. The duck lay without moving. The voice of the raven had the same permanent feel, now, as the crystal chimes of the brook. If the Merganser could stand it, a magpie in the raven's own tree could not. He tried calling back at the raven, pumping the sounds with his long green-shining tail; then darted up from his snag as direct as a dragonfly. The raven, many times his size, left the branch and went sailing away, so black in the glare he looked white.

The Merganser stood up. She was unsure on land, for her legs, better for diving, were placed too far back to support her horizontally, and too far forward to let her walk upright. She half-lurched along, putting her feet on the earth as if fearful of losing her balance. But she soon reached the pond. For a short way she breasted the sunlit ripples. Then she sprang with a short curved cut, deep in a dive, and streamed over the bottom, cleaving the water with the impetuous speed of a creature escaping.

With feathers all tightened and wings pressed to her sides, she was slick and tubular, like an eel. Her webs stroked together and shot her ahead, stronger with one foot when she wanted to turn, but her tail also steered. She knew well this dim glossy world, its wavering plants and the fuzzy stumps of trees that the beavers had felled when they built the dam. She was spinning among them, slippery and dry in her oiled feathers, with motions as dashing as those of fish. Even if she should graze one of the stumps, or a stone, paddings of algae and ooze had softened all the sharp edges here.

At once the Merganser had seen her brood — fourteen pairs of webs, hung from the top of the pond like suspended bright autumn leaves. She dodged toward a bay, but the young had discovered her. Now they followed her on the surface. Wherever she went, a wide shattering of the silver film trailed her.

But feel herself pierce the smooth water, just clearing the tufts of moss on the bottom, and now through the fronds of the pondweeds; set them swaying. Brush the milfoil; sense the sucked current here after a fleeing chub but don't take him yet. Ah, the small kingfisher, spearing down in a dive, has caught him.

Up for air, under again, and the duck passed a blurry log, noting the trout who lived in a channel beneath it. That was a good home. He had won it the week before, when the pelican captured its owner. The Merganser could prod him out with the hook on the end of her bill, but she would not. That would not be her way. Sometime in a chase she might catch him, though he tasted no better than suckers, bullheads, and chubs, who were slower.

A quick dash from the dam to the backwash, over the silt, over the shingle of pebbles, then the pink and white, green, black, and mica-bright rocks, clean-scrubbed at the brook's mouth; on into the backwash, over the brown muck and among the rubbery stems of the water-lilies, too dense; circle around to the pond again.

Once more up for air. Arc through the top of the pond and down under the film's dusty mirror, grown still as the wind died in late afternoon. The sun, sinking below the split fan of a cottonwood tree, spread a swift shade on the water. Now the depths of the pond were darker. The green frosty shine on some of the plants still was showing, and there, in the black

mass of crowfoot, were the gleams of small dusky dace. They were too insignificant to interest the mother, but why didn't the young ducks dive and catch them? They could; they knew how. But they labored along above her, preferring the greater effort of following for the food that she might provide.

She might as well start to work. Listen . . . that scraping sound was a bullhead, rubbing one part of his gill cover against another. Where was he? The Merganser began to search, but ahead saw a long-nosed sucker, nibbling up crumbs of leaves, torn from the water-plants by the waves of the last few days. He'd be tender; he had the big eyes and deeply forked tail of a young fish. She raced after him and he sped away, but the duck was faster, gained, reached his tail, was up at his side, and as he dodged, darted under and snapped her slim pointed bill on his throat. Its sharply toothed edges had fixed themselves in his flesh. He thrashed, as she sprang to the top, but could not tear himself loose.

She had risen too near the white pelican! . . . and could not dive away, for her breath was spent. The pelican jabbed at her with his beak, which was as long as the duck's whole body. He struck so fast, so aggressively, that she could do nothing but·drop the fish. He scooped it into the flopping orange sack under his beak and swallowed it. Unable to dive, himself, he could catch only the fish that swam near the top, which a sucker did not often do. His light blue eyes glittered in triumph.

The young mergansers rushed forward around the duck, so eagerly that the splash of their feet and wings rained upon her. Their hissing cries filled her ears. She flung her head, whipping her crest, and then, lunging out of the water, slapped back on the surface with flattened webs, spread her wings, and went hydroplaning across the pond. But the ducklings also could hydroplane well. They came skittering behind; when she coasted down to a stop, they again swarmed around her.

The Merganser was beginning to sense that the brood would not feed and protect themselves until she abandoned them. Although she might walk away from the marsh, the leaving would have been easier when she could fly. An older mother had had better-developed instincts. Before her molt started, she had gone to a spring she knew, deserting her brood, who could catch their own fish by that time, if they would. But they had attached themselves to the young Merganser, who already had five of her own.

The seasons moved over the animals' unplanned days and gave them a large rhythm: food and shelters changed, and new urges rose. In the diving ducks the nesting impulse came later than in the dabbling ducks. Moreover their young were hatched with strong legs for swimming and hydroplaning, but such weak wings that they did not fly until they were twice as old as the dabblers. They would not have learned when a mother's wings became useless. While her new feathers were growing, she felt as debilitated as a bull moose with expanding antlers; it was not practical then to be foraging for a brood. They should be left, therefore, while they still seemed rather helpless.

But the Merganser was only two years old. These young were her first, and therefore especially late. She had hesitated to break her parent ties abruptly, and while they felt sweet. In another year her tenderness would be better tempered by her own needs. Instinct sharpens with experience.

By now the young drakes were as large as she was, and how spoiled! At least she would make them help. She lowered her head in the water, so that her eyes and bill, all but her crest, were submerged, and began paddling rapidly. The mother's example touched the young to the right reaction. They spread out in a line and raced toward the east side of the pond and its long-winding bays. Any fish that they saw could be driven into the shallows.

There was the trout, the one from under the log! The Merganser leapt forward, half-swimming, half-hydroplaning, churning the water so wildly that the fish fled in a panic. The small ducks helped to chase him. Where the pond narrowed into the sedge beds, they were across it from shore to shore. The trout surely could not escape. On ahead, though, floated the great white Trumpeter Swan. He watched the ducks come, displeased at so much commotion. The trout swam beneath him and into one of the channels among the willows. A line of mature mergansers would have parted around the Swan and pursued their prey farther. The ducklings were intimidated by the backward swing of his head and neck, the motion that often precedes a lunge. They paused; then a few dived; but the fish had eluded them.

When the Swan threatened the ducklings, instantly the Merganser had paddled forward to their defense. But their failure to catch the trout seemed, at that, partly laziness, a waiting to let their mother make the effort to furnish their food. She turned away from them suddenly, streamed back through the pond, caught a chub, and climbed out on the shore, and ate it herself. The young ones found her and came out too. She tried to slip from their sight through the stems of the reed-grass. Some of them followed, pleading; so she lowered herself on her webs, pulled in her head, fluffed her feathers, and closed her eyes. The ducklings returned to the shore. They pecked up the insects at the waterline; one found a salamander. As night came upon the marsh then, they all went to sleep.

Around the Merganser was a hush, as if the earth had turned from activity to awareness. The daytime animals were silent; most nocturnal creatures still waited to take their first cautious steps. Trees and brush were motionless blurs. Only a frail stirring showed in the grasses. The pond's glossy quiet was nowhere touched except by the current's mild, monotonous quiver.

But overhead were vast hints of change — the uneasiness of a lofty wind, and a fine glitter coming upon the sky as the moon rose nearer the crest of the eastern mountains. Though the moon was hidden, its light was pointing across to the Teton rim, where it caught as stars on the crystal glaciers. All dark below was the earth's upward sweep to the high jeweled horizon.

In the north appeared flecks of movement, birds beginning to migrate over the valley. They had rested somewhere during the day, when they could see to forage, and now had set out again. The Merganser watched them approach. She could recognize some of them, those like her marsh neighbors.

The birds were up in the moonlight, traced with silver. The first to pass were almost too high to distinguish, but their throats folded back and legs stretching behind as long as their bodies suggested herons. And here came ducks, so many that they were combing the sky. The largest, with slim necks and wings, were pintails. The ones flying above them also had long wings but shorter, chunkier bodies — baldpates. Separate, off to the west, were a few ducks with the cleanest lines and the most direct flight. They were her own kind, American mergansers, drakes, whose wings were restored to use earlier than females'.

She would not be going. She was one of the ducks who never left Jackson Hole. But the sight of the winging flocks, the sense of their far destinations, emphasized her own flightless weight. Would she feel more free on the pond, floating? She started to walk to the shore, past the squat puffs of her ducklings.

One of her webs came down on the slope of a stone. She tipped back, her wings flew open — and lifted her off the ground! Before she had realized what was happening, she had soared over her brood and dropped buoyantly onto the water.

She stretched her wings, partly rising out of the surface, to test their returning power. It was not much. The softness of the quills' inner, growing ends made them too limber to be dependable. But they had borne her up. She could not yet fly well, but the earth had loosened its hold on her. She paddled to shore, walked up into the grass again, and went to sleep, filled with a sense of horizons widening.

With the earliest sunlight some of the migrating ducks spiraled down to the marsh. First came baldpates, swinging above the pond in a close flock, as sandpipers would, and then, seeming suddenly to collapse, falling straight onto the surface. They pecked insects and bits of leaves from the water, nervously spinning about, checking their speed, pivoting side to side as their feet braked or pushed. They were followed by pintails, who glided down and along the pond, graceful as blowing grass. Before the gadwalls alighted, they flew around over the marsh to survey each shadow for signs of danger; gadwall temperaments were conservative, like the birds' brown and gray plumage. The mallards arrived with the greatest flurry. Need they splash out such wide wings of spray, and stream so far on the surface, and dip their heads under and up, throwing water over their backs? Or were their motions expressing exuberant joy?

The marsh was aflash with color — the green cheeks of the white-crowned baldpates and the brighter green heads of the mallards; the baldpates' pinkish brown breasts and the mallards' russet; the white throats of the pintails, marked off with elegant sharpness from smoke-brown backs; and each time that a pair of wings opened, the revelation of chalk-white and iridescent blue chevrons.

Till the migrants had fed, they scattered themselves everywhere. They were out on the pond and along its borders. They climbed into the sedges. They explored the meadow. And — too much! . . . three baldpates came trotting up from the shore and pulled out roots of the reed-grass, so near the Merganser that she felt the fibres strain under her feet. She went down in the water.

Dabbling ducks were a trial, adding now to the strain of her days. The Merganser lived in a higher key than they. She was more intense, with her energy focused more finely, except when the dabblers distracted it. She herself often caught a whole day's food in a single dive. The others' foraging, leaf by leaf, bug by bug, must go on and on, noisy and obvious — always those tails swinging vertically skyward and beaks down, as if stones had rolled suddenly from the ducks' bellies into their heads, overturning them. Until they had righted themselves, their feet must throw water-wheels off to the sides.

Or the ducks would be running about on land. Since their legs were placed midway between tails and breasts, the dabblers could balance well when they walked, and spent much time in the meadow. When they were not eating, all but the pintails played, chasing each other, rising out of the water and skating ahead on it, flaring into the air and pitching back down. Meanwhile they quacked, whistled, and squawked. Mergansers were silent, except the young, and their mothers when they directed them. They sometimes fished in a flock and then briefly were boisterous, but their resting was quiet. The diving duck might have taken her mood from the smooth green swing over the edge of a cataract; the dabblers theirs from the brook, with its splash, break, and ever-tumbling sounds.

Earlier, when the dabblers were mated, each pair had its separate territory of shoreline and water, where none of its kind might trespass. Then they had kept out of sight in the canals among reeds and willows. After the eggs were laid in the grassy nests, territories were given up. The drakes, and soon the mothers with broods, came out to feed and loaf in the shallows.

The Merganser had spent that time incubating her own eggs, up in a cottonwood tree. The dabblers' confusion had bothered her more after her ducklings hatched. By then, however, the dabblers were starting south, the drakes first and females and young following. Some of the mallards were staying, as she was, but the ducks that annoyed her unbearably were these migrants from farther north, these disorganized travelers coming in every morning.

And now something, perhaps the equinoctial storm, was making the other birds restless — those along the backwash yesterday afternoon, and today even the dignified trumpeter swans were out foraging early. The sun still was clinging to the eastern horizon, but a fluttering, gabbling, and splashing already cluttered the marsh.

She flew away. Her leaving was as simple as that, simple but not easy, because her new quills were lacking in tension. She must beat her wings faster than usual. When she rose from her first morning dive, her infallible brood met her. Springing out of the water, she went hydroplaning along the backwash, thrashing her wings now, instead of holding them level. She felt herself rise, saw the pond sink away. At last she was in the air again. Beyond the backwash was an isthmus. She crossed it and was over the Snake River, wild, swift, lonely.

The animals have found uncounted ways to use the materials of their world. Warm air does not rise for the benefit of hawks, but every column of heat streaming up from a sagebrush plain holds aloft soaring wings. Rocks will weight beaver dams, hollow logs can be lived in and drummed upon, mud will plaster a nest. And see what a river can do: add its velocity to the pace of a creature's swimming, double his speed, send him forward so fast that only the marvelous eyes and nerves of a bird, perhaps, could weave past the rocks as rapidly as the Merganser was doing.

She had alighted in the current and first paddled upstream,

taking into her senses the flow of the water supporting her, the blue-green flow whipping past with a murmurous thunder. It was a violent force, destructive unless met with skill. The Merganser knew it well: how to swim in its pounding pressure, how to seek the slow strands when she wanted to paddle on top. She remembered these things, but she had been away from the river all summer. Something in her must tighten, sharpen.

She was ready. With one motion diving and turning, she was darting downstream in the torrent, under the surface, thrusting her webs against an already-racing flow. As she used the push of a tail wind in flying, outstripping it, so she outstripped the river.

At the first curve, around the marsh, she swept to the outside of the channel, past an island, where the flow was quickest. The river straightened beyond and she swam down the center, since the greatest speed was now there. She must test her strength, prove that she still could keep cool, still make the flashing choice of routes as she spun through the current.

But this plunging ahead was for food, and the prey rode at the edge. There, a whitefish, holding his place where the river will funnel insects to his mouth! On a slant the Merganser swung toward him. He made a tortuous dodge and almost escaped her. But the paired saws of her bill clamped his tail, and she drew him out on the bank.

She gulped him whole, head-first — a treat, for no whitefish were in the pond. She would be quiet, now, till the good meal digested. While she waited, she made herself comfortable. She shook the moisture out of her feathers, fluffed them, and sat on her feet among moss-leveled stones.

In all her view was no other duck. She looked down at the braiding flow of the river. Its motion, ever changing yet ever the same, could put a creature into a trance. On the opposite bank was a line of thinly spaced cottonwood trees, and beyond them the flat valley floor, bright, with an early-morning freshness, yellowness, on the sunlit sage. Shadows of the trees stretched nearly across the river. They seemed bands of dark, submerged plants, separating spaces of emerald water with gold dust suspended in it. The sky had a clear bright depth, with no surface to its blue.

Three cool white and gray gulls flew upstream, in and out of the sunshine. Gently a breeze was shaking leaves out of the cottonwoods. At the far edge of the plain a black moose cantered along the base of a butte. The earth seemed to be poised at some fine center of balance, at an instant that might be forever.

The Merganser began to preen. She drew single disarranged feathers out through her bill, brushed her closed bill across her breast and sides, finally rose and pulled all of the feathers up and then down, to layer them.

Lightly she glided into the water. Paddling upstream in the easy flow near the bank, she made a pleasant time of the journey back. The breeze-blown ripples, running against the river, helped her progress. She saw several fish, a whole school of dace and small trout at the mouth of a slough, and noted without conscious thought where they were foraging. She was not hungry, nor tired, and no duties prodded her. She had nothing to do but sense the lovely wild day and her own wildness a part of it.

Reaching the wooded island across from the marsh, she entered a small bay on the west shore. Enclosed in it were a beaver house and the end of the beavers' canal. During the previous winter the cove had been the duck's base, and it would be again. To float in this arc of shore and feel the water eddying in from the river was a home-coming. Looking across the river, she could see the willows that bordered the marsh, the marsh where her brood were now. What were they doing? Exerting themselves, at last, to fish? The ducklings would not drop from her consciousness in half a morning.

She dived and searched the rocks of the river-bed for a taste of the insect food that she knew was there: caddis and stonefly larvae, the kinds found in streams. One caddisworm had spun a net, in which he had caught some of the travelers in the current, water-fleas, bloodworms, and tinier plants and animals. Nourished by these, he had grown large enough to be a bite for the duck.

But she was not hungry. She climbed the slope of the beaver house to rest on its roof of smooth new aspen timbers. Here, paddling up the river, one behind another, came three drake mergansers. They were old acquaintances; indeed one had been her mate. But now the season had changed; the ducks had entered a new cycle, a different mood. They were interesting to each other but only as other mergansers, not much as males and a female.

The drakes had been through a time of strenuous feather-growing. To prepare for their flightless month, they had acquired a female's colors, in which they had been less conspicuous while they could not escape on their wings from predators. Now, since they could fly again, they were changing back to their glossy green heads, dark backs, and chests and bellies of white with a salmon bloom. They were halfway through the second molt, crowned with green and rust feathers, mixed, but they had no sense of looking fantastic. As they passed the cove, one kicked a vermilion foot, splashing a fan of spray, an accomplishment that the female would find impressive next spring. Then it would rouse the competitive instincts of the other drakes. Now it was but a playful urge, such as a windy autumn day stirs in many birds. The female blinked; nothing more. By the time the drakes were out of sight, she was sleeping.

A sound woke her. Even before she identified it, it had made her uneasy. It continued, and she began to listen. Across on the marsh a raven was squawking. In his cry was excitement. The tone meant that something was happening. Something alarming? A hunter dangerous to her brood?

She flew off the beaver house, and, forcing her wingbeat to its utmost, crossed the meadow and came down on the pond. She saw nothing to alarm her. After a dive, she rose and again glanced around the shore. It looked peaceful — no! Behind her, floating near the beaver dam, was an Otter, enemy of ducks!

Where were her young, who could not fly away from him? The Merganser sped to the end of the backwash. The brood had liked to loaf there but were not there now. She took off from the top of the pond and circled the meadow, the sedge beds, the willow thickets. Near the shore of the meadow, was a break in the reed-grass. She dropped lower. Between the straw blades she could see auburn heads.

The Otter was swimming and splashing; he did not seem aware of her. Yet she must be cautious. She came down in the grass, back several lengths from the shore, and went forward stealthily till she reached her brood. Under the waving seed-heads she found them, a huddle of frightened ducklings. She clucked a low note that drew them close to her. Others came lunging in through the grass. They were awkward. Their legs were not made for smooth fleeing. But they must not go to the pond. Only on land could she lead them to safety.

She started back through the meadow. They followed. To hide, they were holding their heads as low as they could and often tipped forward, righting themselves with flaring wings. They stumbled over the cobble-stones, and ever were losing their mother. One did not find her again. Walking was very arduous for them. They would have liked to rest. But the duck ahead urged them along with the danger-note that she had not used, now, since they were downies. The trip for her, too, took immense effort. The meadow was broken with moose beds, and she must lead the ducklings around them. She must try to keep them from straying away, as well as manage her own clumsy webs.

Finally they passed through a line of willows, crossed a bench of moss and scouring rushes, and came to the riverbank. Beyond was her chance for freedom. By her next move she abandoned it.

Calling, she glided off into the river and paddled to hold her place near the edge. The bank was not high, and the ducklings, eager to be in water again, followed her willingly. As each came down in the current, he felt for the first time a driving pressure against his webs. The feet grappled with it; they knew what to do. Like most young mergansers, they had been reared in a pond, but instinct would have sent them eventually to the river.

Although heavy, the current was weakest here close to the bank. Ahead was the crossing — through a push so powerful that some of the largest animals, even elk, had been carried away by it. The mother would try to take her brood to the cove in the island shore. Fortunately it was somewhat downstream. Their course would allow for a slight drift, but not much. Below the cove the island shore was too steep for a duckling to climb.

Nothing would be gained by postponing the danger. The Merganser paddled forward into the pressure. Its drag on her own webs was pulling her out of line with the cove. She speeded her stroke. Could the stiffening in her muscles be an example, communicated to the small ducks that were tossing behind her?

Most of them were putting all their energy, all their stamina, into meeting the terrible need that they sensed, to follow their mother closely. But three let the surge take them. With motionless webs they were having a giddy ride. The Merganser swung down and attempted to guide them back. They obeyed with a spurt of effort but could make no headway against the current. Perhaps they were swirled into gentler water and found some estuary or slough. Their mother could do no more for them. She must return to the larger group, who were beginning to scatter.

Another duckling was lost, but she was able to lead all the rest to the cove, where she anxiously urged them to climb the sloping side of the beavers' canal.

The young ones settled down among lupines and asters, stirring mildly, safely, in the yellow light under the trees. For a while the ducklings were too exhausted to move. But when one wheezed out his hunger plea, several others joined him.

The mother, standing at the point of the little bay, was looking down into the river. The ducklings would have to have adult strength before they could catch their own fish in such a strenuous flow. She raised her wings and made a flying dive into the green depths of the channel.

The Moose

☼

By the day of the autumn equinox nothing remained in the Moose's thicket for him to break. Trampled over the ground were leaves, stalks of monk's-hood and Hercules parsnip, and fallen cottonwood branches. The earliest light touched the splintered ends of the boughs, and the white snags on the trunks from which they had been stripped.

Among the victims paced their conqueror. Anger was gathering again in his eyes. Soon — now! — he must have the feel of shattering something. He lowered his head to thrash a branch already split from its tree. But his antlers entangled it, and it swung with them. He threw it off, tried to beat it. Once more it caught and was lifted. Still no snapping wood gave him quick elation. He stomped the bough. When he raked it the next time, it broke, for one foot had happened to pin it down. Parts of it flew to all sides as his brow tines tore into it.

The blows of his antlers, of the new fine-tempered horn, clanged through the dawn with the splendor of combat. The Moose was a master; again his nerves were assured of it. He turned from the tree, running carelessly, hoofs scraping the logs. Then he slowed to a walk, and his breathing quieted.

But rage still unfocused his eyes, and the hair on his backbone stayed up. When he came to his woodland pool, a mink's dive distracted him. He let himself down the bank into the water, with his motions now showing the ease of a milder mood.

During the summer his energy had gone into the growth of his antlers. But for several days they had been full-sized and shorn of their velvet, his muscles had been enlarging, and instinct had been goading him into mock battles. The fighting had taught him the length of his forward prongs, and the width of the horn plates above his shoulders, which could be tilted and used as shields. He had grown skilful in swinging their weight.

Once into his real conquest, he would have no interest in food. On this morning however hunger sent him out in the pool. The water was clasping his legs with warmth, or it seemed to, since the air was brittle with autumn cold. And warmth was rising upon his belly and throat, as mist curled from the surface. He stopped, with his long legs sunk deep in the muck, and dropped his head.

Under the water he grazed mostly by touch. At first he found nothing. Months ago he had cleared out the scouring rushes along the shore, and the milfoil. No lank, tender pond-weeds were left, no leaves or stems of the water-lilies. The pool was only a small overflow from Cottonwood Creek; in his long summer here he had eaten most of its nourishment.

He closed the slits of his nostrils and probed in the ooze. The end of his nose, of his muffle, was almost as soft as the ooze itself. It scooped in the feathery muck, touched a firmness, pressed, and the object suddenly crumbled — a decaying branch. Groping forward, his muffle could feel the ooze eddy away from his slightest push. Mass of minute living things, it seemed inert, like a velvet dust lightly lying beneath the water. But a clam shrank away from his lip, and a fleeing scud brushed it.

He found a cord in the muck, the root-stock of a water-lily, and his muffle closed over it as a hand would, testing its size. It would make a bite. His teeth cut off a length, and he brought his head out of the pool. Water poured from the bowl of his antlers, down his shoulders, nose, and neck, and rained back in the pool as he chewed the root.

Here night still left its shadow. But over the sky spread a crisp and delicate shine, and, back in the woodland, bars of sunlight were hanging in gilded dust. Soon a shaft of the brightness cut out from the shoreline trees. It polished the gloss on the water and sharpened the circlets of ripples around the gnats' feet and the minnows' noses. It gleamed on the wax of floating cottonwood leaves. The Moose slapped his ears from his neck to cheeks, and a rainbow spanned his head.

He lowered his mouth for more root. In summer no sunlight, except a few broken patches, had reached the pool. Admitted now by the thinning leaves, milky rays penetrated the water. The Moose saw a muskrat swerve its dive to avoid his brow tines. A swimming garter snake passed in smooth scallops, watching him with its hard little eye. Suddenly flinging his head up, the bull stood for an instant with tightened ears and a quivering muffle. New, long, sunny paths opened out through the brush. They would lead to a beaver marsh he remembered, to a gathering of moose, to combats, and to mating.

Instinct said, *now*.

Pulling his hoofs from the muck, he sloshed toward the shore. He did not leap out but found footholds in the bank and climbed onto dry land, with his fur draining sheets of water — a creature who looked like some giant prehistoric beast, rising from the swamp of an ancient epoch.

He was starting into a world where all other creatures were small and most of them sleek. Grotesque in the twentieth-century wilderness was his huge nose, a thick down-bent column; and grotesque were his ponderous shoulders, his massive hams, belly, and chest, and the string of limp hairy skin, his dangler, that hung from his throat. Among modern animals he would seem an outsider — until his great power struck. When he would rear, and his front hoofs would drive down with a weight equaling that of six large men, his body would seem the suitable one and all others insignificant.

His seemed the right one now, as he trotted away from the thicket. For he ran with a smoothness that erased every impression except that of power. His immense bulk, the color of wet loam, was blotting out here the sun-splashes on Cottonwood Creek, here the reddening fireweed, here the aspens' shimmering yellow flakes. His long legs swung roundly, lifting him over brush, over logs, with no break in their rolling rhythm. He cantered on buoyantly in the white autumn sunshine, in the airy light which had come under the trees.

Hear the wake of sharp sound that follows his feet in the brittle leaves. Hear the crack of the wind-sown twigs under his hoofs. Neither is loud enough. He dips his head as he goes, tearing into the brush. He will not stop to demolish it; he will sweep through the woods like the wind itself, propelled by an equinox in his heart.

He could not bugle his coming, as an elk does, but his noisy approach would convince any rival that he was a mighty bull. Other moose would be challenging with a like commotion.

What caused the whip of that fir bough? Some pulling mouth had released it. He circled the sound, as quiet now as a fox . . . and discovered a mule deer, browsing. The deer was a buck in his prime, yet was only as large as a moose calf.

The bull started on, but slowed at a rustle. Plodding along the path was a porcupine, swinging its tail to shake the quill rattles. To give up the path was not the bull's habit. He hesitated. On came the porcupine, seeming bored, isolated from other animals by their respect. The bull stepped off the path widely.

Other sounds tensed his nerves with impatience. The rising wind churned the trees, tossing down branches. Some broke on the ground like a challenger's signals. The bull listened too for the call of a cow moose. Once a thin moan sent him hurrying forward. But the sound sagged away in a lifeless shudder; it was only the rubbing of dead wind-blown boughs.

The marsh lay in the flood-plain where Cottonwood Creek joined the Snake River. To reach it, the bull was paralleling the creek. His ears followed its running, murmurous over the cobblestone bed. When the hum broke and brightened, splashing through boulders, he was nearing its mouth.

The trees ended abruptly on the west shore of the beaver pond. The bull walked out on the bank. Sunshine fell on his muffle, and sun-bred thistles, goldenrod, and angelica crowded his ankles. Here the shine of the sky lay at eye-level. The pond was a luminous sheet, edged on the opposite side by a flat water-meadow and willow thickets. Beyond the willows hung the band of light over the Snake.

This was a home-coming. He knew the sounds of the wind ruffling the pond, the splash through the beaver dam, and the chirp of the incoming brook. He found the same cries associated with his other great days: the quacking of ducks and the drakes' gentle answers, a kingfisher's clicking, the calls of a raven flock, and the honk of a heron. With a familiar fine-fading whistle the wings of mourning doves bore them past. Here it was, the sound-picture of his marsh, all except the Swan's voice and, most important, the plaintive whinnies of cows and the rumbling assertions of bulls.

But proof of their presence was reaching his muffle. He turned toward the dam. The wind, streaming from that direction, seemed mostly bull-scented. Signs of a cow and a calf drifted confusingly from the backwash above the brook. He snorted, announcing that a very strong bull had come.

At this marsh he had triumphed on three past years. Three times he had found a mate and defeated his rivals. Here had been the sweet commencement of his winter companionship. Unlike the deer and elk of his range, he never had tried to form several cows into a harem; nor did other bull moose. They could not, because their cows would not stay in a herd. But apparently the bulls themselves liked small-family life, for each remained with his mate until the following spring.

Eight years old now, this bull stood at his peak. This was his turn to be one of the few in their prime. This year should be the autumn of his most spectacular conquest. Give him his victory; let his climax be splendid!

From a dead cottonwood in the dam, the Osprey dove for a fish. The sound could have been a moose's head plunging in water. The bull started forward — but reared, alarmed by a sudden, immense flash of white. He wheeled and raced back through the trees. The light had been only the flaring wings of the Trumpeter Swan, taking flight from below the bank.

But their spread was as great as the length of the bull himself; the Swan was supreme among the pond's birds, and could unsettle the arrogant Moose. When he regained his poise and turned, he could see, crossing beyond the tree trunks, the white pacing wings. And he heard the Swan's call spread above the plain, tones with a lingering resonance, clear and deep.

A quick fury seared the bull. He was upright as if he rose on a pivot. Then he threw his weight downward, and the paired points of his hoofs dived into the soil. He lowered his antlers to plough it — but froze. For the scent of a cow moose lay fresh on the earth.

He followed her back through the trees, trailing her by trying to sharpen the pleasantness in his muffle. All the way some of the odor-sensation was in it, but he reached ahead for the splotches of stronger scent on her footprints and on grassheads and leaves that her legs had touched.

The cow had walked into the wind. Here, though, her track reversed. The bull knew that strategy. Now probably she was near, resting where the wind would carry the scent of a follower to her nose. He came to a clearing and found her, rising from the reed-grass at his approach.

She was lighter in color than he and in his eyes was small. But like him she had gaunt legs supporting a mound of curves, and a dangler below her chin, and a huge, fleshy muffle. She looked as if all her parts, separately made, had been joined in haste. Even when she began to trot, circling the meadow, no grace unified her into a smooth-flowing whole.

For giddiness tangled her legs. The stiff lengths of her shanks were flung out, then together. Her head, having no antlers to balance, loosely tossed. Her ears fell across her face.

She was trying to play. As a calf she had sparred with her twin, hoofs striking soberly, but they had watched uncomprehending the spirited bounding of fawns. Full-grown now, the cow suddenly wanted to frolic.

Her clumsiness did not repel the Moose. He ambled her way, and she edged aside into a thicket. He stomped a clover patch. She came out and knelt, nibbling a pad of moss. He reared into a fir tree, hooked his upper lip over a branch, and chewed at the needles. She left the meadow. Beckoning, there ahead in the grove, were soft gleams where the sun slid along her fur.

He lost sight of her, but her scent guided him toward the pond. He heard the rattle of slipping gravel as her hoofs descended the bank, the water's gulp as she stepped into it, and the splash of her swimming. The bull then was speeded by a sound poignantly meaningful, a moose song of forlorn feminine longing. From his throat broke an answering grunt.

Again a wistful wail spread through the air. He must reach that call! But it did not come from his cow. When he emerged from the grove, he discovered that a second moose stood in the shallows.

The bull listened while the musical whine wavered to a high note and drained down, ending with a sigh. The head of the singer swung, dropping then into the water. Her eyes were under the surface, but her ears flicked at each of his snorts.

The first cow splashed up to the other, eyes glittering; she would drive her away. The singer ignored the threat. The sprightly one waded out of the pond, onto the water-meadow, and the bull swam across. She gamboled off, he at her heels, toward the willows beyond the grass. But the sad, irresistible song coiled once more through the marsh. The bull returned to the pond. He was checked when the singer made a quick move into deeper water.

He saw now that she had a calf with her. It was hidden between her muffle and chest. The calf was no reason to give up this appealing mate; more often than not, a bull moose shared a cow's company with her young. The bull paused, and the mother stepped away from the calf.

A whinny wound from her throat. The calf was her first; she had been talking to it all summer and had learned how to let her emotions come out in appropriate sounds. Now with sighs, cajolings, squeals, and small whimpers she invited and rejected the bull. His voice was more crude. After a year of silence it rumbled forth in hoarse groans, grunts, and snorts.

But how intimate was this play with their voices, how tantalizing! The bull was becoming impatient, so the cow strolled farther into the pond. She was nearly submerged, all but the rolling line of her back and her steep lowered neck. The bull wanted none of the pondweeds in which she so easily took an interest. While he waited, he jerked his nose around to dislodge a fly from his hip — and remained with his head reversed. For over his back he saw the other cow enter the pond again.

Sedate now, she crossed it and climbed the bank. The sun richly burnished her curves. The bull followed her out of the water but hesitated when she ran into the grove. After she vanished, the wind blew her scent to him, and the sound of her feet, falling among the dry leaves.

She would not come back. The bright beat of her hoofs called him, yet he stayed at the pond, held by some instinct's light restraining touch. He wandered along the bank restlessly. Now he had lost the leaves' last, far crackle. It was sharper in ceasing than when it was real; and suddenly, then, was a sound heard a long time ago, was a part of the past, of an old, familiar weight.

Noon approached. The Moose lay down in the reed-grass above the bank. From below rose the voices of the mother and calf. The bull swung the smooth-balanced heaviness of his antlers toward the talk, but he did not call. By staying here he had chosen the mother instead of the single cow. For the present, however, he had urged her as far as he could.

The straw tasseled grass-heads were shaking in the wind's quickened pressure. Faster now was the slap of the ripples along the bank. The Moose rose and paced the grove. He thrashed the brush, but the best of it already had been stripped. His antlers stabbed through yielding leaves or thudded on boughs too stout to break. They beat into thimble-berry stalks, which fell with a whisper, not a fine crashing.

Where were branches that cracked as if lightning shattered them; *where was a rival?* Once the cow had accepted him finally, other bulls would leave at his merest threat. This was the time to prove his superior power, now when he had a hope to defend, not yet a reality that all moose would acknowledge.

The wind seemed to sharpen the very light. A blizzard of seeds and leaves drove through the boughs; shadows flew. A distant roar warned of a greater wind coming. Down from the mountain sides rushed a vast sweep. It surged out on the valley floor, straining the sagebrush, nearer and nearer, now into these trees —

Havoc crashed. At the lower end of the pond, branches split and broke. Water violently upheaved. Springing back in a half-crouch, the Moose waited. He was ready for an attack, but no bull appeared, so he cautiously reconnoitered.

The wind had uprooted the Osprey's tree, wrecking the dam. A large bough striking the bank, then the splash of the trunk, had sounded like some huge animal tearing his way through brush and plunging into the pond. The Moose advanced on a wily course, from fir to cottonwood trunk, from hillock to cluster of sunflowers. When he came to the shore, he did not notice the break in the dam, nor the fallen tree. For he found what he had expected — another bull, drawn here by the illusion that he too had been challenged.

The newcomer was young, not quite grown. He had keen points on his brow tines, but narrow plates. The great Moose would dispose of him quickly. He made a bound forward, ears back, snorting threats. The small bull stomped the earth, boasting his own strength. Grunting in real anger, now the mature bull slashed a fir. The stranger tore into an aspen. He was recklessly confident. The older Moose speared the soil, showing how deeply his brow tines cut. He would not gore the young bull if he would retreat, and he would eventually, but not yet. Rage burst through the large bull's restraint, and he charged. The small antler cleverly tilted its plate. Horn clanged on resonant horn until every bare bough seemed to pick up the clamor and ring with it.

The bulls reared and pawed for each other's chests. Hoofs cracked together and threw both off balance. First back in the air was the larger Moose. He reached full height, struck down — but did not descend. For his antlers had caught between boughs of a cottonwood. He was held upright, hind feet on the ground, with his neck in a tortured arch.

The small bull was puzzled to have the fight stop so abruptly; he wandered aside. The captured Moose lunged up frantically. He could rear higher, and lift his antlers above the boughs' crotch, but they wedged again at his forward drop. The stranger perceived that his great opponent was helpless. He made a few strikes at the brush, waited, sniffed at the ground for some scent he might follow elsewhere.

A beguiling wail edged through the grove. The cow, no longer hearing her friend, called to him. The bull trembled. He tried to snort a response but was choked by the weight on his throat. Once more he hurled himself upward. He could not escape from his trap. The young moose knew now what to do. He hastened away to find the cow.

The half-strangled bull had sagged downward. He was losing strength. But he suddenly threw all his effort into a final lurch, and one of the imprisoning branches broke. He fell to the ground. He lay there until the tide in his inner force turned, tried to rise, again fell, but finally got his hind legs straightened up under him, and his forelegs. A few unsteady steps took him along the shore.

He heard a splashing across the pond, in one of the channels among the willows. Swimming over, he saw the cow walk out onto the grass. The small bull was behind her. Energy rushed back into the weary Moose. Hurling spray, he plunged toward the intruder, who gyrated into a startled leap. The bull pursued him, and the younger one bounded away. He ran swiftly along the pond's backwash, around the end, out of sight.

When the Moose routed his young rival, fury made him impressive. Actually he was weak from his ordeal. Returning to the shallows, he let himself down, with water covering his belly and legs. He gave every fatigued muscle its way. His head drooped, and he closed his eyes. For the present he had no slightest impulse to seem powerful.

The cow and her calf came into the pond to rest near him. The cow shed small murmurs as she walked. They might be an accompaniment to her motions or might be a kind of conversation. The bull did not answer. He took an expansive breath. His heart was trying to build his strength quickly. At each beat ripples pulsed away from his vast black sides.

The pond had smoothed, for the wind was only a prelude to the real storm and died soon after it wrecked the Osprey's tree. The valley was shadowed by thunder-blue clouds. The air had a dark clarity, like that of water, in which the rocky pinnacles of the Tetons showed polished and sharp.

All the blown seeds found the earth. Even the aspens were quiet. Ears were searching the hush for a marmot's whistle. *Whistle*, pause, *whistle:* that shrill warning had piped out all summer, whenever clouds gathered. But now the marmots were underground, entering their winter sleep. The swans in the sedge beds floated motionless except for their watchful brown eyes. A school of minnows held their formation without a quiver.

Soon the air in the valley was shot with a chill. And something more ominous was occurring. When the Moose first lay down, half his dangler was submerged; but the water had fallen below it. A band of wet fur on his side was widening. Through the break in the dam, the pond and its channels — the home of these many and varied creatures — was draining away.

One by one they became alarmed; but not the bull. He was rested now, and his companion absorbed all his interest. Her eyes were clouded with sleepiness; how could he stir that quiet mood into action? He pulled a stalk of exposed milfoil from the silt but let it hang from his mouth uneaten, while impatience rumbled rough in his throat.

The cow rose. She walked up a drained bay of the marsh, the calf following. The bull accompanied them, after the calf. That precedence was a moose custom. The cow stopped for a mouthful of willow leaves, and the bull crowded close. Lightly she brushed her muffle along his side. At once, though, she started on again. Snorting a protest, he fell in line. Her reluctance was like a willow barrier, seeming impassable until the fall of its leaves, one by one, showed the breaks in it.

The mother led through the reed-grass. She would cross the backwash to the bank on the opposite shore. This part of the pond, empty now, had become an expanse of drenched, oozy silt. She took a step into it, felt it pull at her hoofs, with a straining leap reached the other side. The calf walked out onto the mud. It captured his legs before he was halfway over.

The cow called from the base of the bank. The calf worked his thigh muscles but could not drag himself out. Soon the silt rose to his belly. His mother's voice became urgent. He looked at her desperately and still struggled, with his effort evident in his neck and eyes.

He sank lower. His chin lay upon the silt. Great snowflakes began to fall. They melted when they came to rest on the mud, but they lay white on the calf's coat. He blinked when they dropped on his lashes.

The snow was coming down faster. It whirled in the air so thickly that even the cow had no clear view of what was happening. A raven flew up the marsh and began to circle above the backwash. Five others came, gaunt, shining black birds that banked and dipped. They hoarsely called, drowning the mother's bewildered moans. Through all other sounds were cutting screams of fear. One, then, was smothered. It was the last cry of the calf.

The bull rounded the old shoreline and met the cow as she climbed the bank. She sensed that her young one had perished, and was filled with a great, tormented confusion. She started to run away. The bull pursued her, his hoofs springing against the earth. At last he was not restricted to moose talk and to slight, cautious advances. This was a good, real chase, welcome to his masculine strength.

The rise and fall of her dark hips led away through the snowy mist; her hoofbeats summoned him with a softened pattering. She was starting north, away from the grove, up the flood-plain of the Snake. Why so rapidly? She was running surprisingly fast. And why in such a straight course? In her flight was no dodging, no coyness. Did his instinct know suddenly, or did the fact slowly clear, that she would continue as long as he followed? How did he become aware that actually she wished to leave him?

Now his feet merely were dropping upon the earth, not driving against it. He slowed to a walk and wandered aside to the river. On the bank he stood with his eyes turned down to the water's gray lifeless rush. If the cow had repelled him because she was tired or hungry, he would have sensed the reason and waited until time overcame it. But grief for a calf was something he had not experienced. He could not understand that another emotion might interrupt her friendliness; that if he stayed near her, grief, like fatigue, might pass.

He walked about aimlessly, until there was no more daylight to shine on the snowflakes, until they were only a white chill, sifting down to lie deeper and deeper about his hoofs. They stopped falling, and the clouds parted long enough for the sunset to cast a pearly radiance over the valley. The bull's bewilderment seemed to lift. He would find the trail of the cow and join her, not too insistently.

His muffle would guide him. It moved over the clean new frostiness, searching back from the river, well beyond the line where the cow had passed. Lifting his head, the bull sniffed the air. In its tang was no trace of her scent. He hunted over the ground again, slowly returning to the river. Her trail should be here somewhere, surely. And here it was, but the snow had covered it.

Perhaps the marsh was, after all, the place that the Moose remembered. The cow might be there, still making her amiable sounds for his ears. Scents on the wind might promise clashes with other bulls. When tomorrow's sun rose on the shimmering pond, everything might be right.

He went back. By the time that he reached the marsh, night was thickening in the valley. The grove, though, looked wider with snow on the ground. All the tree trunks stood blackly distinct, holding aloft an intricate feathery cloud of white boughs.

Instead of the pond, a hollow dropped away from the bank. This was an alien marsh. More snow fell. Soon the night was too dark to see it, but the bull felt the flakes touch his muffle, and heard the small tinkle of crystals alighting on crystals.

At first he walked through the grove, senses alert to each sound and scent. As he found no sign of the cow, he moved less, but increasing stress tightened his eyes. His mood was slipping into an anger heavier than his quick mating temper. This was the same violence he felt in late winter, when the cold had lasted too long. Perhaps he associated this first snow with bitter days to come; more likely frustration had roused his viciousness. Misfortunes were mocking his conquest.

Through much of the night he stood at the edge of the trees, over the Beaver's house, the mound of mud-plastered sticks built against the bank. The Beaver worked on the dam, using willows from the opposite side of the pond. Finally sounds below the Moose drew down his ears. He heard a vague brush of movement, teeth chiseling in bark, and the fall of chips. The leaves of a young tree were shaking, and snow from its boughs was thudding onto the snow beneath. The Beaver had changed his methods; he wanted stronger timbers and was cutting an aspen sapling.

For a while he gnawed persistently, was mysteriously quiet, seemed to be pushing about under the trees. He found a stick previously cut and dragged it to the pond. He returned to the aspen and gnawed again, went away, and came back.

All the stir deepened the bull's moroseness. For he was a creature to whom work had no meaning; he never had made a shelter, or stored food, or fed young. The Beaver's sounds might be caused by strange animals; they kept the bull in a tension. With a swish, then, the aspen went over. It lay with its top extending out from the bank.

Though the storm had been stripping the grove, leaves still clung to this sapling. The Moose went down into the half-empty pond, where he could browse on them. Their strong pungent flavor was the first real satisfaction of the day.

For a short time the Beaver was silent, troubled perhaps by the movements of the bull. But the mending of the dam was urgent. He began to gnaw the trunk of the aspen, to sever the top. While he chiseled, the Moose continued to eat the leaves. The Beaver finished his cut, grasped the end of the shoot in his mouth, swung it around and down the bank, and started to the dam. What was this: was the bull's food being drawn away? He walked along, catching a bite but resenting the interference.

Even while he had his teeth on a leafy spray, the Beaver dared to tug at it. Up on his hind legs shot the Moose. He would stomp the infuriating Beaver. But the Beaver dodged the hoofs and fled to his house. He was a vanishing shade in the muddy pond, lost now in the mound of sticks.

Not lost! The bull will get through to him. The Beaver will take all the fury the Moose has had no chance to release.

The Moose would break down the house by trampling upon it. He reared, but the roof was so high that his weight could not give all its drive to his hoofs. He would tear off the top of the mound with his antlers then.

Bracing his forefeet on the wall of the house, he raked his tines into the rubble. He flung the upper branches away, found the next layer entangled, cracked them, tore them out, hurled them aside. All his terrible power was freed now for violence. Ears were flat on his neck, he was gnashing his teeth, and his mane stood stiff, bristling, a black halo above his strength.

Wildly impatient, he was stomping the wall. His hoofs found the air hole where the thatching was thin. They pounded it, broke it through. Many times they beat down on the weakening timbers. Almost at once the front of the house was flat, blocking the entrance.

Part of the roof stood firm, spanned by a long, club-sized bough. The Moose slashed it but could not loosen it; it was wedged in the lower sticks. If he had pulled them from under it, he could have removed it. But more than instinct is needed for a systematic plan. What could he do now? Though most of the house was down, he had not reached his victim — unless, as might be, the creature was crushed. The bull could smell open flesh.

As the Moose thrashed at the beam, his energy started to scatter out. His blows were losing their aim, his antlers sheared off the mound. Even the small, peaceable Beaver had thwarted him. He charged up the bank and pounded along the shore, out of the grove, away from the marsh, onto the broad, white, flat floor of the valley.

The dawn was only a grayer night, wider, emptier. Cold puckered the moist lining of the Moose's muffle. He was walking along the bench west of the Snake. The river, below the plain, flowed in a tree-lined channel between cobble-packed walls. A mist of crystals, frozen fog, drifted along the cut. Otherwise nothing stirred except the cloud of the Moose's breath.

The monotony of his gait swung his dangler, and his head was borne down by his antlers, which seemed more a weight now than a weapon. He was threading between the sage clumps, not topping them with elastic steps. He was sunk in a gloominess that often overwhelms moose — so typical of them that human beings once gave them a name meaning *misery*, and believed that they die of the slightest wounds.

No animal argues reassuringly with himself, or designs ways to overcome his misfortunes. On this morning the Moose could not tell himself that his recent defeats all had been accidents. He could not visualize a new summer, with crops of succulent water plants, nor another autumn gathering of moose. Instinctive living, which is passive, blindly guided, denies hope

to the wild ones. But most animals look forth with an energy that is almost eagerness. It had collapsed in the Moose.

He finally stopped and lay in the snow at the top of the ledge.

Over Sheep Mountain curved a bright golden line. The line became a disc. A crust of shine covered the white dome, and then the sun was above the ridge. Around the jagged high rim of the valley every east-facing cliff, rock, and canyon-side was a flake of light. The frozen mist over the river became a drift of sparkles. A glitter dusted the frost on the sage, the seeding flowers, and the edges of the birds' feathers.

A magpie flew past, turned, and came to perch on the Moose's back, tucking its toes into his coat for warmth. A weasel bounded by, white-furred in a world at last also white. From a tree down by the river rang the neat, decisive taps of a hairy woodpecker. The cold was enlivening the animals' movements and their voices. The Moose should have been making his boast with the snapping of brittle boughs and the clang of horn.

The river-wind spun along the ledge. Its sound could have been the lament of a wistful cow moose. Curiosity was so low in the bull that he did not investigate — or should he? His ears stiffened as the whine seemed to sharpen into a song.

He rose and stood listening. The new, more melodious sound came from upstream. He walked toward it. Over the ledge appeared the muffle and then the shoulders of the calf's mother. Now she had reached the top, and her sad call wound over the plain.

Was it a call to him, or a song of grief for her young one? At the very sight of the bull, again she might flee. He went forward slowly, still meandering through the sage. The first sign of any returning confidence in him was a grunt, hardly more than a thickened breath. The cow's head turned, and her song stopped abruptly.

With knees lifting higher, the bull began to trot in a straighter course, over the brush, over the mounds at burrow-holes. He tossed his antlers, and their ivory plates flashed in the sun. She watched him coming. When he was near, she bounded sidewise, as if she would bolt away.

He approached more cautiously, stopping when he was a length from her. There he raised his head and blew the breath out of his mighty chest. He knelt, ploughed his antlers, and threw their load upward. Moving ahead on his knees, he hurled a shower of snow. He rose and beat right and left in the sage, spreading its spicy fragrance.

He was magnificent, all his power stirred with rage. For he was deeply angry, now, at her reluctance. He turned and walked a few steps, seeming to leave. Did unwillingness relax in her then? She made no visible move, but the bull swung around, and she did not start away, not even when he came and with his own nose touched her muffle.

On the Water-Lily

THE CLEPSINE LEECH

THE LEOPARD FROG

THE PHYSA SNAIL

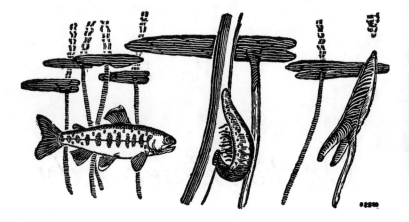

The time had come again for the Leech to find some animal whose blood she could take. Only a single day had passed since her last meal. She had fasted many months when she had no young to feed. Now thirty infant leeches were attached to her under side by the suckers on their tails. They could absorb their own food if it came to their mouths; they were almost old enough to leave her. But they still received some nourishment from her. While the Leech was cradling offspring, she gave the substance of her life — she who existed by requiring that other creatures give her theirs.

Always half-transparent, she showed this morning that her chain of stomach sacs was empty. Yet she rested, quiet on the water-lily stem. Whenever she began to wander after sleeping, the first move that she made was sharp and sure. Other animals might waken stretching, yawning, fumbling to their feet. The Leech would wait until she could make her start with the determination necessary to her kind of hunting.

Lying on the smooth bare stalk, she looked like a willow leaf, one fallen into the beaver pond from the brush along the shore.

Thicker than a leaf, she was about the same size, tapering shape, and green-gold color. She had fitted herself to the roundness of the stem with her young, like pale soft tentacles, pressed down beneath her. Two suckers, one on each end, clamped her firmly.

But she was ready for the hunt. Lifting along the stalk, she waved the ribbonlike length between her suckers with a fanning motion. It was a panting, just as clearly as the heaving of a chest is. The Leech was a curiously expressive animal; the way that her elastic, simple flesh would change its shape with any impulse, to protect, enjoy, or injure, was emotion naked.

When she had taken oxygen enough, she loosened her forward sucker. No shadow of another creature fell across the eyes upon her back. But the Leech did not trust eyes alone. She reached out from the other sucker for the touch or flavor of living food.

Her motion seemed a probing in the water, not an idle groping. It brought her first a threat. The taste of a trout came to her lips. The fish, a tiny one, had seen her and was hovering near. He stopped with a fascinated gaze upon her side, and twinkled his tail in expectation. Speeding in, he closed his mouth on one of the young leeches, snapped his head to pull it off, and was away to eat it.

The mother clutched together with a start. She arched her sides so deeply that her little leeches were enclosed almost as in a tube. Then, swaying back to the stem, she lay along it, covering her young.

But fear, though quick to rise, is quick to fade in a creature like the Leech. Soon she was only hungry. She reached up to her utmost slimness, twice as long now, stretched her mouth-end sucker higher on the stalk, and fastened it there. Her other sucker made the step and attached itself behind the first. She looped out, swinging with a bounce when her two ends came together.

Immediately she took a second step and others, measuring her way along the stem with a rhythmic speed. She was passing physa snails. They were a favorite food, but their shells were drawn down close around them as they rested, and anyway she may have sensed that she would come to more of them. The snails in the pond were like the mice on land, so numerous that a predator could almost always catch one.

There ahead a snail had begun to move. To limber himself, he had raised his shell and was swinging it upon his back. The Leech preferred to clamp her mouth on a snail's flesh, just be- hind the head, but now she could not reach that far. She caught the spiraled tip of the shell with her forward sucker.

At once the snail knew that his shell was gripped. He tried to pull it loose. His foot was stuck to the lily stem with a heavy mucus, and the Leech was clinging with her hind-end sucker. The two were pulling at each other. The snail was throwing his shell from side to side, but gradually the Leech began to drag it back. Then with a jerk she snatched the snail from the stem. They swung out into the water, angry creatures fling- ing themselves about from the Leech's rear attachment. The snail still struggled in a frenzied effort to whip his shell loose from her grasp.

Her hold was too secure for him. She coiled herself around him and clutched him firmly, as in an arm. He groped out from his shell, yet trying to escape. Without unwinding, she slid her mouth from the point of the shell to the open edge and up be- neath it. Now she could fasten her mouth upon his shoulder. From the center of her sucker's vacuum cup she thrust a tube, a piston, deep into his flesh. The tube was like a hollow spear, through which she could pull out nourishment.

Unrolling herself, she hung down in the water with the snail attached to her free end. It was difficult to drain the fluid from dense tissues: she must suck in pulses. As her throat contracted, all her body helped to pump. She squeezed herself from tip to tip, relaxed while the liquid ran back into her throat, and squeezed again, a labor that half-curled her upward. Her color brightened, and the rows of white spots on her back became more sharp from her exertion, or perhaps from pleasure.

The snail would be a small meal, not enough to satisfy the Leech's hunger. And yet she checked her sucking after a few full draughts and gave the prey to her young. Again she rolled herself around the snail, this time in such a way that his flesh was brought against the little leeches. She did not draw her tube out of his shoulder, but she stopped her pumping. She was quiet while the tiny mouths attached themselves to his skin and began to pull.

Although the mother was partly curled around the snail, she held him loosely, so that she looked protective now, but she was not enfolding him with love. She waited until all the small throats had been filled completely. As the young ones finished, they would swing away from the snail and lazily stretch out from the clutch of their tail-end suckers on their mother's flesh. She may have felt their motion; when they were through, she seemed to know. A bit of nourishment was left for her. She started the pulling in her throat again. Each pulse was gripping the snail up closer to her. She rocked him as if she were putting him to sleep, as indeed she was.

The dreadful lullaby finally ended. She drew her piston out of his shoulder, straightened herself, released her forward sucker from his flesh, and let him fall. He began to drop through the water, slowly and softly since he was so light now. With his blood gone, he was colorless, a little pale ghost, swaying weakly from the rim of his shell as he reached for something, possibly life. But all his firmness left him suddenly with one of his breaths. He shrank back limp in his shell. Numb and probably in no pain he had drifted out of consciousness before he touched the silt.

Apparently the dulling of the Leech's hunger gave her a sense of exquisite ease. She turned and curled about in the water smoothly, with motions seeming to express delight. Her mouth pushed out until her throat was slender and then wound back, as an elephant's trunk does, slipping slowly along her skin. She brought the mouth up over her young ones.

Her forward sucker rose upon the stalk and fastened there. Becoming still, she hung from her two ends in a loose loop. The little leeches were exposed. Dark with food, they also seemed content, for many swung about with motions like their mother's.

The Leech would rest for a while. Not long; soon she must find another victim. Autumn had come, the time for her to hibernate, to creep among the rocks at the shore, where ice would freeze around her and protect her from the sharper cold of the winter air. Before she went to sleep however, all her stomach sacs should be tight with food.

She would have liked to lie, slung here from the stalk, until the dark of night. But the little trout prevented her. It had not taken him long to chew and swallow the infant leech. He had returned. And all the time that the mother was fighting with the snail and feeding herself and her young ones, he had been a thrilled spectator. He had darted around them, had hung in the water tense and bright, then snapped to a better place. Another small trout, recognizing his excitement, sped up to discover what was happening. He too would have liked to watch, but the first fish would not let him. He chased the other off whenever he approached.

Now . . . the mother was quiet. And the little leeches were extending themselves to their full length, spreading up from her belly and out in a fringe along her sides. The trout shot up, stopped, twitched off one of them.

The mother may have been asleep. She did not seem to know. More and more of her young were lost, until the trout was so full that he could not swallow. But the huge meal did not make him sleepy. Like a vibrant imp, he saw a chance for mischief.

He would bite the mother, not for food but fun. It took more time to rouse his nerve for that attack. He eased up to her side but backed away, swam up again with alternating waits and spurts of motion. Suddenly he nipped her.

The mother jerked and again was still. Once more he pricked her side. Aroused, she may have smelled him in the water, for she swung around and flattened herself on the stem. But the trout had found a game he liked; he nicked her even there.

She would leave the torment if she must. Sliding now, not looping out, she climbed the stalk. The trout stayed near but did not touch her while she was in motion. And the Leech forgot him, for above her was a great windfall, the resting Leopard Frog.

His chin was on the water-lily leaf, and his belly, plump and pearly white, was bulging down from the surface of the pond.

One forefoot clung to the stem, but his hind legs floated out. As the ripples passed, they swung his legs away from his sides.

The Leech would attach her sucker in the thin skin of his groin. She climbed until she was close beneath him. Slipping her mouth across his belly toward the hollow under his leg, she clamped her sucker.

The Frog jerked all his legs up to him. Quickly the Leech thrust in her piston. It went into an artery — good fortune! For sucking was easy from a tube of flowing blood.

The leg above her twitched about, but the Leech clung fast. The Frog kicked off from the water-lily pad. He was swimming energetically, wildly, but the Leech was drawing great deep mouthfuls. She scarcely was aware that she was racing through the pond.

She knew, though, when a heron caught the frantic, careless Frog. With an upward sweep she and the Frog were out of water, into air. The belly and the hind legs of the Frog and the Leech were now inside the bird's beak. It was dark here, all but the slits along the bill's half-opened sides.

But what a pity; the Leech was going to lose her fountain of blood. The Frog was struggling and little by little was working out of the heron's mouth. His legs squirmed forward, and the sharp edge of the bill scraped off the Leech.

She lay at the side of the heron's tongue, and was becoming conscious that this, too, was flesh when the heron tossed the Frog to try to catch him lengthwise. As the bird flung back her head she swallowed. In a swift black ride the Leech went down the heron's throat.

It was the kind of death that a leech might want, decisive and quick.

A morning came when the Frog looked out from his nook and found a skim of ice upon his puddle. All summer the puddle had not dried or flooded, since the Beaver kept the water of the marsh at always the same height. Reed-grass grew in the little pool. The down-bent leaves had traced their liquid circles while the Frog sat underneath. But on this day the stalks and the points of the blades were all held rigid. The wind, which could not sway the imprisoned leaves now, shook them stiffly.

The wind had blown all night. It whirled away the warmth of the ground so fast that dew had had no chance to form and freeze. And the dawn seemed colder with no frost to catch its small stars out of the early sunlight.

The Frog was crouched below the stone that roofed his nook. His throat was soft, because his breaths had kept it pulsing. But the moisture from the glands upon his back had frozen, so that he had a new and sharply brittle skin when he awoke. He broke it, like a skin that he needed to molt, by hunching himself and puffing out and squirming. But he did not eat the skin of ice.

The cold was something definitely there. A creature almost felt that he was being watched. The Frog had made himself compact and still, as he did when he was trying to escape a hostile eye; but the cold had found him. He should not risk one more night here in his cranny.

His eyes were standing high and globular, not pulled within his head as when he slept. He saw the sunshine tilting lower and lower through the grass stems, finally to the mat of runners on the ground. Above the stems the loosely hanging seed-tops were a fluff of light. A flock of small birds flung themselves down through the grass. The birds were chirping in excited haste as they foraged, juncos and chickadees for seeds, the yellow warblers for drowsy insects. Their wings were snapping open and shut to balance them, and their feet continually grasped new holds as they slipped on the smooth straw stems. In a little gust the birds had left the grass and swept away — so limber.

There at the base of a gentian, sunlit whiskers glistened with the motion of a sniffing nose. The red-backed mouse was out for a meal of seeds, but first he must be sure no other animal was out for a meal of him. And the Frog could see the Varying Hare. The Hare was nibbling at a clover patch. For several weeks she'd cropped it. From habit she kept moving back in the narrowing shade of an aspen sapling, although she showed more sharply in the shadow than in sunshine, now that her fur was white. The chickadees, the mouse, and Hare could spend the winter in the meadow, for they had their own warmth. But the temperature of the Frog went up and down with the heat or chill surrounding him.

Cutting and chewing were motions that the Frog had never tried, but he recognized them as eating. Watching the Hare, he pulsed his throat more deeply, as he did when he discovered food. And soon he heard a fine dry scraping, surely an insect's chitin plates. No leopard frog would jump for a sound alone, and when he saw what caused this one, he looked away. It was a pinch-bug. He had swallowed those and quickly had disgorged them, for they took an agonizing grip on his stomach. The Frog learned slowly but remembered well.

The stir of any small thing was intriguing, even the bit of thistle-down, caught on the mud, that twitched in the breeze — a mayfly? He dragged himself out from his nook to see, and found a bombardier beetle, popping with anger at an ant that grasped its foot. If the Frog were warm he could have reached both insects by unfolding from his hind toes in a long swift stretch. But his legs were nearly as stiff as the ice-bound grass.

The runway of the ants and the beetle's hole were in his view and well-known to him. On a fireweed stalk he saw the damselfly who often rested there, her glazed wings upright. Behind her the leaves of a willow blew in the sunlit sky. From the willow through the tops of the grass to the cottonwood tree, and from the tree around to his nook and puddle were the boundaries of his summer.

What he was seeing now he knew as well as his tongue knew how his mouth was shaped: the single thistle, spiny-leaved and rigid in the swaying grass; the wild-rose bush where lady-bird beetles gathered for the aphids; under it the feathers molted by the swans and stripped of their down by mice; a weathered furry foot, left by a mink when he caught the mother of the Hare. None of these things had fed or sheltered the Frog, but they might be dear because they were familiar.

The sight of them was being awake — out of his winter coma, able to hop through the meadow, catch delicious insects, sit in the sun-warmed puddle. Another frog, at the entrance of a different cranny, would look at different things and those, for him, would be the feel of his days. But for this Frog these things here in his eyes were summer, the only part of the year he knew. How could he leave them now without a sense of loneliness for them and for himself?

He must give up the ground on which he sat. It was molded to his plump wide belly, the forefeet that he braced below him, and his hind legs, backing to a point; it fitted him. Even better, because it gave him safety, was the stone above his nook. The stone was glossy-smooth, for a glacier had rolled it here. Beneath it he had slept or lazily watched for insects out in the grass. He had found the stone the day last spring that he came ashore from the pond and the mating assembly of the frogs. The nook had been his home, but he must find a shelter where he would not freeze in the winter so soon coming. Any day he might drift into his long sleep.

The sun had loosened his rigid legs now. He must not wait. He lengthened in a low hop toward the pond, a hop off at a slanting angle, and one that bent his course again; his trail would be confusing to a follower. Each time he landed with no thud or crackle of dry leaf. Few birds hopped as softly. He stretched so smoothly into the next jump that he seemed to flow through the grass stems with a motion like their blowing.

Beyond the grass he reached a little bay, a glossy shadow under willow boughs. Beyond were water-lily pads, splashed by the glitter of the pond. He stopped beneath a mat of bedstraw — dark, but flowers of light, reflected from the ripples, quivered among the leaves. Here he was hidden from tall enemies like herons, though not from any animal on the ground.

A shrew discovered him at once, but she was busy, probing into a snail shell.

The Frog would stay in the bedstraw briefly. Unlike active animals who chase their prey, he moved from wait to wait. Looking down to the cove, he saw that whirligig beetles spun delirious circles there, a way to dodge an enemy, perhaps a frog. Water-skaters rocked in the leaf-drift at the shore, as if the wind had blown them to it while they slept with their long thin bodies slung from their overhead knees. They were still; the Frog might catch one. He pulled his hind legs close to make a leap. But the skaters were awake. The breeze flung down a spider from the willow, and every skater jumped. They clambered around it, fighting for the prey.

Beneath the cove raced small, round, light-rimmed shadows cast by the dimples under the skaters' feet. The marks on the Frog's skin were exactly like them. The bright lines bordering his dark spots even were metallic. The background of his smooth skin could become as brown as the mud instead of green, as now. If he were in the ooze among the dimple-shadows, no eye could detect him. He should dive.

Before he stirred himself, a garter snake slid out from the willow roots. The snake moved over the wet-shine of the muddy shore. Her sensuous grace was hiding her readiness to flash out in a strike, but the Frog knew. Gulping air till he was nearly twice his size, he now was twice as hard to swallow. He stopped the pulsing of his throat and held himself with a stillness so uncanny that he had the look of being unreal, simply not there.

The snake was followed by another. They swung around, advancing toward each other with their heads up and their forked tongues flicking in and out. They came together and the tongues touched. Drawing back, they dropped their heads to the ground, slid forward close to each other, and then coiled together intricately. But one unwound and glided down the shore.

For a while the snake lay in the cove, her tail beneath the ooze, her body slanting up, and her head and neck above the surface. At long intervals her head would sway beneath the water, forward and out again with a sultry rhythm. A sharp blue-bodied dragonfly skimmed around her. It hung a few lengths off; then darted toward her face and hovered just beyond the reach of her tongue. The snake made no sign as again and again the dragonfly shot up on its stiff wide wings and abruptly backed away. But the dipping of the snake's head finally became faster. Once then, when she submerged, she swam away.

The Frog looked back to find the snake left on the shore. It too had disappeared. In light low arcs the Frog leapt over the beach and into the water. He dived beneath the ooze, his puff of silt dispersed, and not a trace remained of him. When he left his summer life, he would be leaving dangers as well as satisfactions.

His hibernating urge was seeking just this, darkness and the feel of being covered. But instincts may conflict. He still was hungry. He pushed above the ooze but saw no prey. His eyes were somewhat like a human's, focusing in air, near-sighted in the water. He sprang to the top, to lie with his chin on the glistening pad of a water-lily and a forefoot holding to the stem.

The ripples passed as quickly as the current of a brook. He

gave himself to the motion, spreading the webbed toes of his hind feet, letting the water catch them and float his legs out from his sitting-on-his-belly posture. A sheet of the water flowed up over his back, to part around his head and stream together at the point of his mouth. He pulled his eyes in half-way, and the inner lids rose on them. But the lids were clear. Through them he could see that a long-horned leaf beetle had alighted on the pad. He slowly raised his eyes, one at a time, and opened them.

The beetle had come to lay a clutch of eggs. She chewed a hole in the leaf and, standing with her back to the hole, curled down the tip of her abdomen to stick the eggs on the under side of the leaf. Besides hers, clusters of several other kinds of eggs were there. The beetle was not even a water insect and, when her young hatched, they would have to pierce the lily stem and live with their heads inside to breathe the air in the plant. But while the eggs were in the water, it would cushion them, would keep them from drying out, and protect them from extremes of heat and cold. The water of the pond was not alive, but even better than the land it cradled life.

Would the beetle fly away if the Frog should move up closer? No need — here, curving over the edge of the leaf, was a physa snail, a nourishing meal when his stomach juices had dissolved the shell. The Frog unfolded his sticky tongue and shot it out to grasp the snail. He swallowed the mouthful, using his eyes to force it down by lowering their bulges into his throat.

The snail would still his hunger. This was a pleasant way to end his summer, resting on the water and the sun-spilt leaf. But soon a numbness in his side felt wrong to him. He clutched his legs up to him. The discomfort became sharper. He groped with a hind foot, tried to scrape away the frightening sensation, but could not reach it. He dropped the stem and kicked out, swimming one way and another. Soon he felt a faintness.

A Clepsine Leech had attached herself to his groin. "A thieving leech," her name meant, and with her sucking piston fixed in his flesh, in an artery, she was taking blood from him in great draughts. Trying to lose the Leech, he dashed through the water, scarcely caring where he went, and did not see a great blue heron.

The heron watched him coming. Her snakelike neck had folded back to bring the point of her long bill close to the surface. As the Frog came springing past, she stabbed for him and caught him crosswise.

Instantly his skin had sweated out a thick and glabrous fluid. It helped him to squirm ahead, although the grip of the heron's beak was strong. His thrashing, violent and convulsive, made it hard to hold him. She clamped her beak still tighter. His thighs worked out of the edge, but his feet were inside. If she cut through his legs, she would lose the Frog. She lightened her bite a little. He flung himself from side to side. She would do what she did with a fish, toss up her prey and try for a lengthwise catch.

But the Frog was better at dodging than most fish are. He hurled himself out past her shoulder, sliced through the water, on down into the ooze. He was safe from the heron — and safe from the Leech, for he had scraped her off in his struggle in the beak.

A fright is exhausting to a creature. The Frog lay deep in the mud, now breathing only through his skin. Perhaps here he should allow the last thin thread of consciousness to break. Yet something did not satisfy him. The ooze may have been too loose a cover. He began to crawl ahead.

The floor of the pond became more solid; under his feet was a fine silt rather than the spongy ooze. Beyond the silt he walked on hard-packed rippled sand. A different kind of water was draining over him. With no good sense of smell he could not tell that it was fresher, but it gave his skin more oxygen, and it had a quick beat, not a smooth flow like the undertow along the ooze. He was in the current of the brook that filled the pond.

Very sleepy, he was going where his feet would take him. That course was not a blind one. His feet had touched a shingle and were turning always toward the larger pebbles. They next found stones.

The Frog had left the pond and now was moving up the brook. The water was warmer, for a passage underground had given it the temperature of the earth. Even the cold of winter in Jackson Hole did not reach far down into the soil; the brook would never freeze.

The Frog's need for a cranny in the stream-bed here seemed almost like an ache. He crawled along in a daze but did keep going, feeling for any crevice that would hold him. Approaching a rock, his cheek slipped into an opening. A heavy hind leg dragged up, pushed, and he went in farther. The nook was not quite deep enough to enter, even in his flattened hibernating posture. But sand was under it. He squirmed down, scratching with his feet until he had a hole that held him snugly, covered by the rock. At last he could stop moving. Feeling snug and satisfied, he had a last say for that summer, croaking under the water with a sound like pebbles being shaken in a little resonant skin drum.

His eyes were closed, but he could feel the gentle flow of the brook. All winter it would smooth his skin, while he was . . . sleeping. The regularity of the current dulled the touch of it. Now the only thing he sensed was the rock above his back. It was a stone . . . like the stone roof . . . of. . . .

What other creature's life was so unsettled as the Snail's? Each time that he might begin to feel at home in his world, it changed. The Swan pulled up the pondweed where he hatched. He fell to the bottom silt but found a bur-reed he could climb. A muskrat carried the reed away. The first thread that he spun down from the water's film was broken by the frisking Trout; and hungry enemies were always diving, darting, or prowling toward a snail. Harried by so many shocks, what could he do except ignore them? He glided around the pond as unexcitable and patient as if he always got the thing he wanted.

That was his way. It had kept him alive through all the sum-mer. Now, at the time of the equinox, he was three and a half months old, and suddenly there was a change in his habits. The cause of it was in his feelings, in himself.

He wanted something that he never had known, a touch, a taste, or a sight. He hardly could have anticipated what it was; it would be strange but good. The new impulse, the urge to search, awakened him before another snail was stirring.

Food might fill his emptiness, although his need was not exactly a hungering. He had spent the night on a water-lily stem, and the stem was nourishment. He pushed his shell up higher on his back and lowered his head beneath the edge. He scraped a mouthful of the algae coating from the stalk. Apparently it was not satisfying. He ate down into the firmer tissues of the stem but took no more than two bites. Food could not still his longing. He lifted his head and rippled the muscles in his foot with a waving motion, front to back, that sent him forward.

This was not one of the mornings when he must hurry to the top of the pond for oxygen. At dusk, before he entered the pond, he always filled his air sac. All night he would inhale from it. When the water was warm, his breathing was fast, and he would start to suffocate by dawn. But this night had been cold, and so he had a good-sized bubble of air in the sac. He wandered up the stalk, slow but continually moving. Whatever he sought could as well be on the stem as any other place.

Neighboring snails were resting here. He turned aside for the grown ones but was gliding over the smallest, molding his foot above them with a touch so delicate that none was pushed aside. He might be the only snail awake but not the only creature. The Leech was looping up the stalk. In a quick, determined way she stretched ahead, attached her forward sucker to the stem, and swung her other sucker up to a hold behind it. If her mouth should drop on flesh, how swiftly she would clamp the sucker tighter! She overtook the Snail and fortunately passed him.

A bloodworm there above was active too but seemed more frantic than the Leech. With his rear feet caught in the stem, he fluttered out through the water like a streamer whipped by the wind. He let go and began to swim, one end and the other curling in a dizzy winding and unwinding that took him no-where. It might be a way of breathing; but in a few days he would leave the pond to become a gnat, and then he would dance above the willows, yet obsessed with motion.

The Snail curved over the bloodworm's tube of mud. His gliding was so smooth that it looked like stillness. The rippling in his foot was hidden against the stalk: he was here . . . then simply was there, although he had made no visible movement. In the earliest light he seemed a twisted strand of the night itself, with his purple-black shell and his flesh, the color of darkness. But soon the rays of the sun were pointing down the stem. They showed the Snail as clearly as the scarlet bloodworm.

A thump on his shell has ripped him from the stalk! He is falling to the pond floor! As he dropped, he was struck again, and the new blow set him spinning. He landed, bounced, and came to rest with the point of his shell turned over on the silt. He shrank up into the spiral so that all his flesh except the sole of his foot was covered — but his nerves jumped, for his enemy nipped it. To save himself, the Snail must risk another bite. He pushed his foot out, spread it on the silt, and got a grip by pouring out a sticky liquid. Then he swung his shell upright and sucked himself down into the silt. His enemy left. It had been a young trout, one too hungry to wait for the soft black flesh to expose itself again.

But the Snail had lost his bubble of air! The blow on his shell had bumped it out. Now he had no more oxygen to breathe. He pushed up out of the silt, discovered the lily stem ahead, and glided to it. Stifling, he climbed as quickly as he could. As he neared the top, he swung his shell from side to side, a desperate motion stimulating to him. At last he reached the surface. Turning over, he hung for a while from the water's film, with the opening of his sac up through it and the fresh air seeping into his blood.

He did need food, if only for his search. He moved up onto the lily leaf. Ripples were slapping under it, to lift and drop it, but the Snail was used to being swung and tossed. He lowered his mouth to the leaf, and his tongue rolled back and forth to scrape off bites with the hooklike teeth along its top. He rasped the bites against the horn plate in his mouth to grind them smaller, and then swallowed them. Although his body was oddly shaped, a spiraled mass that fitted the turns of his shell, its workings were like those of his neighbors, even those of a great black moose.

The moose stood near him in the pond. She also was eating water-lily leaves, was grinding and swallowing them, enjoying the same flavor as the Snail. The Snail could hear the spill when the moose's head came out of the pond. He could see the sun flash on the water draining from the furry cheeks. If he could have reasoned, he would have been alarmed at the moose's foraging, leaf to leaf, but nothing frightened the Snail until it was a touch on his feelers, a shadow sweeping toward him, or the taste of an enemy in the pond. Not fear but restlessness made him go on.

He moved to the side of the leaf, there drew his body out of his shell and flattened it into a flowing sheet, and curved down over the edge. A part of him was on the upper surface of the leaf and part on the lower; no animal with bones could pour itself like that. He let his shell trail back till more than half his foot could grip the under side of the leaf, and then he swung the shell below, and after it the pointed heel of his foot.

He would find the object of his hunt in the water, surely. The only good thing in the upper world was an easy breath. The light was too sharp there, especially when it struck the surface and rebounded. And the winds soon made the skin of a creature like himself feel tight with dryness. Down in the pond no glare bedazzled a snail's eyes, and the current's motion was a gentle stroking, smooth and soft as the touch of another snail might be. The fortunate animals were the ones like leeches who could take their oxygen directly from the water. Now, anyway, the Snail had a sac full of air and was in his favorite place, the lower side of the lily leaf.

He generally rested here, but on this day he searched across it. He slid too close to a hydra. One of her arms waved out against his feeler, and instantly her other arms swung over him. His face was pricked with her little barbs of poison; if he had been as small as a water-flea, she would have paralyzed him and lifted him to her flowerlike mouth.

He passed a sponge and felt the suck and squirt as the animals fanned fresh water through their tubes. A ram's-horn snail approached him. She wanted some firm thing on which to lay her eggs and liked the look of his shell. But he was faster than she and drew away. He was moving over the eggs of whirligig beetles, dragonflies, and physas like himself. When the leaf died, it would carry the eggs to the bottom, where they would lie till spring. They would be needed to help hold together next year's web of life, but they were not important to the Snail. He came to the other edge of the leaf with his search still unsuccessful.

He flowed off onto the under side of the surface film, the water's fragile skin. His foot pushed backward — carefully, since the film could break — and soon he had traveled many lengths from the leaf. Small waves were heaving him up and down. One, scattering in spray, tore openings in the film. The Snail lost hold. He started to drop but caught on a gelatine rope, a ladder between the top and bottom of the pond, made by the snails.

He glided down, enlarging the rope by adding a new thread to it. Here came another physa, climbing. The Snail was patient, but he also was obstinate. The stranger should turn and go back down. If he would not, he should be knocked from the rope. The Snail approached the other one belligerently. When he reached him, suddenly he swung his shell out over his head in a thumping blow. The stranger slipped but did not lose his grasp. He too was willing to fight. They twisted and grappled on the rope, each hitting the other with his shell. Neither would give up the way and neither had to, for they could have passed. It seemed that they just wanted a little battle. Gradually they were moving lower as they beat each other. Finally they came to the bottom. They separated, and the Snail set out along the floor of the pond.

Still searching, he toured his range all morning. Toward noon he began to move more slowly, tired or perhaps his urge was wearing itself out. Several times he had been in danger. A snake had saved his life by eating the nymph of a dragonfly that threatened him. And now, as he climbed the lily stem again, the Leech was groping about for food. She missed him, and once more he crept up onto the leaf.

His quest was ended. For on the pad was another physa, young as he and somehow different from all the snails that he had passed. He sensed that he must reach her quickly.

She flowed away to the side of the leaf and started to curl

over. Swiftly her shell had vanished. Coming to the edge, he found that she was falling through the water in a pretty tumble. He too dropped down and landed near her. Righting their shells, they started over the silt.

He caught her under the shadow of the leaf, which fluttered above them, seeming agitated, although it was only wave-tossed. He glided up the spiral of her shell. Smoothing into all its turns, he crossed it, weaving, pressing himself against it widely, as if he could not get enough of its lovely touch.

She drew herself up out of the shell, turned over the opening, and stretched back toward him. He joined her with an eagerness that was almost violence. They moved upon each other, yearning, clasping, stroking. Now their faces were together. He slipped around her with the perfect grace of his fluent flesh, and they found the hold that gave them utmost communion. For an instant then they were still.

They separated with the lightest possible breaking. The Snail drew back in his shell, crept down and away. She found a gelatine rope, climbed to the surface of the pond, and returned to the water-lily leaf. For her that one experience was the only companionship that she would know. The Leopard Frog had stopped to rest on the leaf while she was gone, and at her first appearance over the edge he snapped her up.

The Snail himself had come to an end, but only the end of his young days and his summer. Something in him was complete. Now he could stop not only his quest but his daily foraging and tedious journeys to the top for air.

In his gliding over the bottom of the pond, he reached a small hole, eddied out by the movement of the water. He sucked himself down into it . . . deeper; all of his shell was buried. Still he continued the grasping that took him lower. When he was several times his own length under the silt, he relaxed. Here, in a sleep so heavy that he would not breathe, he would spend the winter.

In the spring he would come out and begin his life again, and perhaps not be so much confused by the longing that was not for air or food. His second summer might be pleasanter than the first, with more and even different rewards for patience.

The Trumpeter Swan

✵

The late, yellowing sun shot its rays through the willow brush. The willows grew out of the water in clusters like giant fistfuls. They met at the top in a wide glinting blur. Below was the lucent brown gloss, now frosted lightly with autumn dust. In flowing water the dust had wrinkled against the stems. On sheltered bays swimming animals had left shining paths.

The Trumpeter Swan was gliding beneath the wilderness of the brush. Where the overhead boughs spread apart, his breast broke a pale blue sheen. Under the leaves that joined, he was scattering green-gold flakes. He was crossing reflections of the stems, red with a violet bloom on the bark. But all the willows were not bursts of color. Among them were dead thickets, bare and silvered by the sun so that they looked ice-coated, tangles with the crystal magic of winter. Any day the sheaths of ice would become real, and the tremulous water no longer would yield to a white feathered bow.

Here the willows became so dense that the Swan must keep swinging to wind among them. He paddled faster, with his throat tensely upright. He could not relax when he felt so enclosed, although he was more concerned for his family, following him, than for himself. A moose and her calf were browsing near on the leaves. They were out of sight, but the plunge of their hoofs was disquieting. And he could hear their talk, rough murmurs that may have seemed a violence to the Swan, whose own voice was a ringing clear channel for his emotions.

The thickets beyond were spaced thinly, and he came out on a small lagoon. His throat fell into a flow of curves, a tranquil sway forward and back over his wings, a lift to capture a mayfly, a downward folding to layer a feather, a revolving to scan the shoreline. The fly and feather and shore may have been only excuses for the elegant pleasure of motions so slowly graceful. He seemed more quiet than if he had not moved at all.

Now, late in the afternoon, little wind touched the responsive water. It was a stillness quick to stir, like the Swan's awareness. But a flock of mergansers splashed into the bay. They were learning how to drive fish to the shallows. The one they pursued dodged away to the willow canals, and several of the ducks dived. The Swan returned to the willows himself. Mergansers, with their habit of swimming underwater, made him nervous. For no one could tell where they would come up again. The Swan had a poise so sensitive, controlling such immense power, that lively animals often were subdued by it. Much of the time he lived in a peace he partly created; but no duck respected it. Nor did the winds. And the snows would not, and even more disastrously human beings had entered it.

He was leading his family to the beaver pond, a width from which they could rise in flight. Since the day drew to its end, his mate might follow him into the sky, if she ever would. Rounding a thicket, he missed the silent movement behind, of the others. He strengthened the stroke of one foot to pivot, and paddled back. His three cygnets had stopped to dabble for insects in floating leaves. Their mother was not with them.

The Swan was patient. He held his place with a weaving pressure of one web and the other and watched the fledglings. Their winter plumage was nearly complete. At first they had been all violet-gray, but their heads now were pinkish rust. Their bills were violet, mottled with rose. And did their colors please their father, whose eyes could distinguish them but were used to adult swans' vivid white?

The cygnets were two-thirds grown, larger than ducks but doubtless small to him. Their necks were shorter-proportioned than they would be later, and their heads were fluffier. One was beating his wings, a stretching that half-lifted him into the air, with his olive-brown feet patting the water. The other two also began to flap — little mimics still. In many ways they were not mature, needing yet to be watched. See how heedlessly they are switching their bills through the leaves, concerned only with food. They have not learned a swan's exquisite caution. At their age most birds were meeting the world by themselves, but in those species the new generation numbered thousands, even millions. The Swan was protecting his cygnets as if he had known that less than a hundred new broods of trumpeters had hatched this year, throughout all the world.

Their mother should not expose them to danger by lingering so. Surely she was not far behind, concealed by the brush, but why not here? Her manner lately had made the Swan uneasy. She had seemed separate, most of the time near the family but not careful to guard the cygnets on one side while he guarded them on the other, not balancing her moves with his, with a matching grace as harmonious as a single swan's; not coming into the air with the others, not once since the young had begun to fly.

No preceding ripple promised that she approached. The Swan sent a light puff of breath through the coils of his windpipe. Two of the cygnets paddled toward him. He called again and the third left the leaves. And then from behind a willow spread a reflected white gleam. Above it advanced a feathered throat and the folded wings of the mother. Her neck was reclining back over her wings, not alertly tall. And her head was averted, with her bill across one of her shoulders. She came too smoothly, for even a swan.

The water was dark in the stems behind her, but the cygnets' wake circled her breast with blending currents of lemon-yellow and amethyst. She entered a spill of sunlight. As it touched her brown eyes, it kindled a flicker; or was the flash from within, an answer finally to the Swan's emotion?

He started on to the pond, and the others fell into line behind him.

Warblers and chickadees whisked about in the brush with high querying chirps. They were hunting roosts for the night and would be anxious to the instant of falling asleep. The Swan glided past them, seeming as serene as the limpid water, yet he probably was more vigilant than the small restless birds. His eyes were sweeping the surface for a wedge of ripples or deep boiling below, signs of a swimmer. Ahead was a silken swirl, no pattern to fear; a school of fingerling dace had turned to retrace their way. The herringbone flow, there, meant only that the channel was draining faster. And the clustered lines, fine as streaming hair, marked but a sunken branch.

The Swan heard the light cascade through the beaver dam and the rhythmical churn of mallards' feet. Among these he listened for sounds less innocently bold, for drops flipped from ears, or water swallowing over the end of a tail. The cygnets were spaced as they should be, between their father and mother, but the throat of the Swan often swayed aside to give him a backward view, for he no longer trusted his mate to sense the rear dangers.

Beyond the willows the family came to the sedge beds, islands of sod. One was their roost. They passed by it and on to the open pond. After several days of stiff wind an unbroken surface lay ahead. It was brushed in the center, but the opposite side was a dark shine that repeated the shoreline cottonwood trees with only a slow, smooth, serpentine ripple rising along the reflected trunks. While the wind was blowing, the Swan had had to take off toward the grove, the short way of the pond, and the run had been scarcely long enough. Possibly that was the reason why his mate had refused to follow him on their flights.

He proceeded along the dam as far as the dead tree that supported its center. There he turned toward the pond's farthest point, at the end of the backwash, and raised his wings. His black webs beat in the water with alternate strokes, and his wings pushed down great cambers of air, lifting him.

Now his feet were striking the surface, now even his toes were above it, now they were folding beneath his tail. His neck was a slim level line, with his black bill piercing ahead. Around him the air poured back, the earth fled beneath his breast. He had passed the shore, passed the aspens beyond, was over the bank of the Snake, and out into the river-wind. Its draft held his weight, and he stopped his wingbeat to give the others a chance to join him.

As he rose from the pond, he had begun to call. This time his mate must follow. His voice wound through the tube in his breast, a living trumpet with coils possessed by no other kind of swan. Because of its length the sound came out deep and sonorous, and clarified to a single pure note. His intense wish made the summons vibrant:

Come . . .

The call spread through the valley below him. It rang on the rocky pinnacles of the Tetons. Long after his breath was spent, the sky and the mountains seemed to hold the tone:

Come . . .

He circled over the bank of the river. As he turned, he could see the three cygnets, earnestly working their little wings. But no great white swan sailed behind them. The father flew back to the pond, too anxious to restrain his speed to the young ones' pace. His mate was floating below, near the tree in the dam. He glided so close to the upper boughs that the Osprey, perched there, drew back his head with beak opened in anger.

Come . . .

The dam drained into Cottonwood Creek, which turned south to enter the river. Over its mouth the Swan swung about. The cygnets made a shallower curve and closed in behind him. The four crossed the dam again.

Come . . .

But she would not.

Alone then, if he must, the Swan would take his young on

their tour of the evening sky. He looked back and saw that his mate's throat was stretched, curiously, along the top of the pond. He never had known her to do that before. To her, the position was a discovery of comfort. While the cygnets did not need her care, she would relax her weakened muscles. Holding her head up, to watch for enemies, took all of her stamina these days. As she waited, she let even her wings droop. The surface partly supported their weight, which she was not strong enough now to lift, much less to lift herself by their beating.

The mother had not been in the air since the flightless weeks of her summer molt. But the Swan's own wing feathers were grown out now; hers should be too. This was the season when swans should be making expeditions around the valley, around the peaks cupping the sky, up the Snake to its highest rill. Always on other years he and his mate had taken their young on autumn flights.

A swan's nature widened as the fall of leaves widened horizons. And these short family tours were the only ones they would make. No trumpeters anywhere migrated southward now. Once they did; even the grandparents of these two had been in the spindrift of wings scudding down the continent to the marshes that do not freeze. But human beings had come to those marshes to shoot swans for their down. And some of the ponds had been drained. Wildness was gone from the south — knowledge that older swans seemed to have given the recent ones. This Jackson Hole pair never had seen the devastation of the wintering grounds; yet their impulse to go was checked.

Actually human beings had stopped killing trumpeters

everywhere. They had found that their spirits were lifted by the resonant voices and the great translucent wings. And so they had made a law that no one might destroy these birds. But how could that news be conveyed to the wild discouraged instincts?

The birds' down kept them warm in the northern winters, but too often their food was lost. They would stay on the narrowing ponds until the underwater plants were glazed over completely; then would starve. So quickly a species can die: of the immense flocks of trumpeters less than a thousand birds, anywhere, now remained alive.

These two had been fortunate. They had been reared on the Red Rock Lakes, where there was permanent open water. Then on one of their fall flights they had found this Teton Marsh, even warmer, and had stayed. Men had come here to kill ducks however, and some of their shot had fallen into the shallows. The mother swan had found several and had swallowed them, believing them snails perhaps. By this time the shot had eroded away, but she was sick of lead poisoning — sick of civilization really, as much as the swans who starved.

The father guided his cygnets northward above the river. Few signs of human beings showed below. At the southern end of Jackson Hole was a town, but the birds could not see it. It was enclosed by three buttes; men had the same urge that animals did, to hide their shelters.

The light over the valley was reddening. In it, here and then there, was the glint of a nighthawk, up for a last meal of insects before starting south. The plain and the mountains were colored more richly, now at the close of day. A mauve shadow had fallen down the front of the Teton wall. It was patched with intense yellow, not sunshine as it seemed, but groves of aspens. Along the base of the slope the dusk lay like blue smoke in the forest of pines.

The Swan would have liked to lead his young ones across the Teton barrier — and out farther, above the wide rolling mesas of Idaho. But they were not old enough. They would need almost adult strength to lift themselves over the bright broken rim-rocks and the glaciers. They could fly above the top of the lower, eastern range. At the head of the valley the father turned back, and the line of four swans followed the Gros Ventre summits, which flowed smoothly beneath them, like a drifted ledge of snow. Beyond were the Wind River Mountains, crest of the continent. Bighorn sheep tracked their peaks, as the keen eyes of the young swans may have discovered. They were other vanishing creatures, like the swans incorruptibly wild.

The Teton shadow range had stretched halfway across the valley. From one instant to the next the swans could watch it advance. Over the plain were moving dark images of Buck Mountain, Teewinot, the Grand Teton. The pale, downy sagebrush had been casting the sunlight back into the sky, but soon the outline of the western range lay on the opposite slope. The brightness was gone from the sage, and into the sky came night's lonely spaciousness.

In the still air the valley sounds rose with a wide clarity. The swans heard a raven call and the beat in the river's pouring. The raven was only a black knot at the top of a dead tree far below, but one of the small swans felt suddenly cold in his heart. He sped forward until he was flying above his father and dropped to ride on the broad white back.

The older Swan drove his wings faster to carry him. Even to lead the young ones, at their slow pace, was an effort. The father was the largest of the valley's waterfowl, and so heavy that he could fly easily only when he flew fast. Alone he would work his wings smoothly, in slight curves, seeming hardly to move them — but a flight that was swifter than eagles'. That was the way he enjoyed sweeping through the sky. But tonight he was up for the cygnets' sake, not his own pleasure.

He crossed over the plain toward the river and the marsh. The small one, seeing that he was going home, rose from his father's back. The Swan tipped his wings in a spiraled glide, reaching the backwash only a little above its sheen. His feet had been lowered, with his toes spread to check his speed. The hind toes touched first, and he flattened his webs forward, sliding onto the water without a splash. His rounded breast sank through the surface and stopped, with ripples swelling away. As soon as he heard the cygnets alighting, he paddled forward to find his mate.

She was floating at the far side of their island roost. Over the stiff points of the sedges the Swan saw her throat, straightened now. It seemed to have lifted her eyes to their utmost height, but when he came in her view, a tilt of her breast raised her head measurably higher.

He and the cygnets rounded the island and walked up into the sedges. The mother stayed in the water. She no longer spent the nights on their hillock; that was one of her strange new ways. The young ones let themselves down on the spongy roots. Sleepiness soon dazed their eyes. The Swan too folded his feet beneath him. He plucked a few sedge seeds and turned his neck backward so that his head lay at the upper edge of one wing. Most of his bill was under the feathers, but his eyes were out.

His mate appeared tense. He raised his head, for she was pushing against the island. With fumbling, broken motions she was trying to come ashore. But her legs were not strong enough to support her, and she sank back in the water. He may have sensed, for the first time, that her recent behavior was due to weakness. Distress crowded a note from his trumpet, and several softer notes, intimate and troubled. She held her head stiffly upright until after the strain of her effort had passed. Ease came first into the base of her neck, which curved onto her shoulders. The relaxation slowly rose, all her throat arched, and she poised her head downward. The motion flowed on, and her black bill swung lower, finally to lie on her snowy breast.

She slept. For a long time the Swan stayed awake, watchful and now with a deep uneasiness. The sky was a merging of faded daylight and coming moonlight, a bright dust that anywhere might be stars. The yellow and green of the shoreline grasses still faintly showed. Their reflection was touched by the shine on the pond, which gave them the delicacy of grasses in spring, when they were tremulous, with their stirrings yet uncertain. Below the vertical blurs the water was mauve and blue-silver, the shades in the sky. A dragonfly passed, drained of his color. The grasses grayed. Overhead then was only a dark immensity, pricked by stars.

The sun long had fallen below the Idaho mesas. But its rays reached the noctilucent clouds, high above the stratosphere. They bent on that ceiling and struck down to the snows of

Mt. Teewinot. The peak stood up rosy and luminous in the night-blue sky, like a live ember.

A new wind brushed the mountain front. It made the whole earth seem uneasy. Even the stars had a livelier glitter. And the alpenglow paled in the space of a breath, as if the wind had extinguished it.

The cygnets started the family out in the morning. Their parents never hastened them away from the roost. Like all trumpeters, they depended for safety on observation, not hiding, and spent the nights on a lookout surrounded by water, which would reveal most approaching animals.

As soon as the sun was up, the cygnets began to stir. Piping a soft impatience, they slipped down in the water and filed away toward the willow thickets. Their father overtook them; more slowly their mother followed. The family passed other sedge hillocks and a corner of the meadow. The sun, coming in levelly, filled the grasses with light, and glanced off the water, striking the swans' plumage twice.

Even the father's own feeding was an aid to his young. The willow channels were ice-bordered this morning, but he paddled along the open center, watching the liquid brown depths. Some plants grew too deep, but finally he found a bed of clasping-leaf pondweed that he could reach. He swung down his head and first raked in the muck. The sensitive skin on his bill touched a dragonfly nymph. He nibbled it up and probed for more. Meanwhile, in brushing between the rippled leaves, he had broken off some of them. They floated up, nourishment for the cygnets. And when he pulled up a whole spray, water-boatmen and scuds were dislodged, and the young swans caught them. Several ducks — mallards and the consistent little thieves, baldpates — sped up to share the food. The Swan did not object. He cleared the channel of the weeds, satisfying his own hunger, the cygnets', and that of various smaller birds.

These days his mate was not taking food. She floated motionless near the others. The thicket shaded her, but flickering lights from the water crossed her breast, touching a frosted sheen, exquisitely white. The swan herself seemed out of reach. In her eyes was the new thing, suffering that removed her from even her family.

When the meal was finished, the cygnets paddled off to the meadow. They were sleepy, climbed out into the grass, and cuddled down. Their mother had stayed in the willows, but their father joined them.

Chances to groom his feathers were rare these days; this was one. He swept his bill down over his throat with an upward fluffing at the sides; then ruffled it across his breast. Turning his neck, he brushed his back and slipped·his head beneath each wing from behind. He seemed to be examining all his plumage. He lowered his throat ahead of him and raised and shook his wings, waving their limber edges. Their shine flashed over the marsh. He placed the wings along his sides, with no refoldings like a duck's, and pulled down his feathers. The preening had been dignified, even stately, with no motions faster than the pace detachment set for a swan.

He laid his head between his wings and closed his eyes. He also wished to sleep, for his day's vigilance had begun too early. Late in the night the Beaver had been moving with sounds that were harmless, but toward morning a slap of his tail had sent a warning over the marsh. Peering up from the sedges, the Swan had discovered an Otter.

The enemy swam about, underwater or sculling through the surface. Moonlight silvered his wakes, and the ripples swished into the sedge blades of the swans' roost. Finally he went away, but he might return. The Swan had felt too alarmed to relax again.

Even now, in the reassuring light of day, he could not sleep. For the weather was making all the creatures restless. As the equinoctial storm approached, the pressure of the air was falling, and the animals' tissues were absorbing moisture. That condition was always a strain. It made the swans, too, nervous, but they did not hop, flutter, or call continually, or fight. They showed their discomfort by letting the others' movements unsettle them. The cygnets were roused by a Varying Hare, thumping her own tension.

At once they wished to be somewhere else. The Swan was disturbed at the prospect of taking them out alone. He called to his mate, but she did not come. Perhaps he could lead the young ones to the backwash, usually a quiet place. No; they would go past the dam. Two parents might have distracted them. They ignored their father's urging. He paddled faster and swung in advance.

Beyond the dam was the wooded bank with the Beaver's canal cut into it and his house built against it. The adult swans never had brought the young here; an enemy could steal toward them too secretly through the grove. Now the cygnets swung up the shore, piping their pleasure in the new place. They stopped near the canal and jabbed for water-skaters in the debris drifted against the bank.

The current, draining toward the dam, was a swifter movement against the Swan's feet than the flow in the sedge beds or thickets. But his webs could detect another, uneven surge, no doubt stirred by the Otter. An otter might swim up under a cygnet and pull it down. He was likely to do it only if he could find no fish, and this pond fairly swayed with fish; yet an otter's caprice was not to be trusted.

The Swan's eyes strained across the pond. The Otter was submerged and not visible through the surface, dazzled with sunlit ripples. The smallest cygnet, a female, sensed her father's alarm. She showed the first stilling of her impulsiveness, the first touch of a swan's caution. While her brothers hunted more insects, she moved farther along the shore, where she could take flight more easily.

The heavy irregular surge became stronger. No more waiting; the father must take his young ones into the air. He called and had made the first leaping strokes with his feet when a marsh hawk swung over the grove.

The Swan could outdistance the hawk in flight, but the cygnets could not. Here then they must stay. The harrier had seen them. He would torment them — a prospect that put a more sensuous grace in his wingbeat. This was one of his great days. The swift wind and the Osprey had given him opposition, and that he loved. Here could be more of it.

With a shrill cry he turned down and straightened out, hanging above the young female. His yellow claws dropped. His hovering face would be terrible to a cygnet; ruffed and flat, it combined the look of a hawk and an owl.

The father was down-wind of the harrier. He could rise only by turning his back on the cygnets. He paddled instead to the little one's side, whipping a violent spray with his wings. The hawk cried another taunt, and the Swan replied with a louder warning. His neck was drawn back and his beak was open, ready for a murderous lunge if the hawk should drop lower.

At a sag in the wind the harrier swayed, lost his position, and circled above the pond to advance again over the cygnet. With that brief break the father sped into the wind, was soon off the water and pursuing the hawk. The harrier swept away, across the meadow and river and on over the sagebrush plain. The Swan was close behind, calling threats. The harrier went into a steep dive, a winding ascent, and another dive — sinuous turns that the larger Swan could not closely follow. But in fleeing, the hawk had admitted that he was vanquished. The father hastened back toward the pond and the greater threat of the Otter.

As he returned, his eyes, always quick to find whiteness, saw the Hare in the tawny brush, the pelican on the blue-black water, and his mate. She was paddling past the dam to the cygnets. The Swan came down as she reached them.

The young ones had been subdued by their fright. Now they would be obedient. The marsh no longer beat with the Otter's swimming, but the family filed to the sedge beds and their roost. There, secluded behind the tall, upright blades, they would wait out this tumultuous morning.

Soon after noon the wind blew down the dead tree in the dam. It crashed on the pond with the high, metallic clatter of shattered water. Ducks exploded from the surface. The pelican sailed away. The great blue heron flopped up with a *quonck* in a loud collapsing voice. And out from the willows, like mosquitoes from beaten grass, rose smaller birds, incredible numbers seen together, of magpies, and mourning doves, belted kingfishers, yellow warblers, mountain and black-capped chickadees, pink-sided juncos, and tree swallows. Only the swans did not fly. Over their hillock the white and gray wings briefly waved; then were folded.

Soon the fears, too, were folded. The boldest birds came down, each leading a flock of excited followers.

During the morning the sky had been brushed with hairy-fibred cirrus clouds, very high. Below them fluffs of vapor now came over the Teton crest. They were clouds so intensely, luminously white that no eye could look up at them with comfort. Even when one had obscured the sun, the others shed a soft and buoyant radiance from their own light. Under it everything solid seemed to lose its weight. But soon deeper-shadowed clouds crowded across the peaks.

The storm was close to Jackson Hole. Now the winds whirling around its center had passed on east. The water lay heavy and still, repeating with darkened colors every shoreline twig and root, every russet, cream, or brown-striped breast of a floating duck.

The Swan's mate spread the clearest outline on the surface. Below her perfectly was reflected the white sway of her side. It ended in the black knob of her knee, high because her legs were pulled up in discomfort. The Swan came off the roost to float beside her, and the cygnets followed. The family drew together, seeming to sense a crisis. A strange new sound was roughening the air.

The first hint of its meaning came to the Swan when he found that his toes touched the muck. They never had done that here. Now his webs were flat on the bottom, and he stood. Then the cygnets' feet touched, as their mother may have seen, for she lowered her own webs. At once she started toward the pond. Not being able to walk, she must stay on water deep enough so that she could paddle. She stopped at the outer border of the sedge beds, and the others with her. But she soon had to move again.

The dam had not been visible from the sedge roost. When the swans came out into the pond they discovered a break in the Beaver's masonry. Around the roots of the upset tree the water was pouring down to the creek below. This was the reason for the roar they were hearing. The shores of the pond were drawing inward; its size was shrinking. Behind the swans were channels and slopes of bare mud.

Several times the family let the shallow water drive them on. Then they went to the center of the pond and huddled there near the end of the fallen tree. The father was facing the backwash, but into his sidewise vision a shadow flowed. It was the Otter, topping the dam with his lilting step.

The mother too saw him. They swung together, enclosing the cygnets. The Otter dived in the pond. But he emerged and began to tour the borders. No switch of his tail-tip and no toss of his arrogant head was missed by the eyes of the Swan.

The Otter tumbled and swam in the draining pond. He rode the cascade through the break and caught a fish and climbed up on the prostrate trunk of the tree to eat it. The swans went out on the open surface.

A second otter came. The lively creatures were splashing together. The swans turned toward the shore, then back on the pond again, for the otters went out on the silt. The father Swan shifted about, tense and frantic.

Over the earth swept a sudden darkening, and a quick wind stirred the leaves. The air was oppressive. It lay in the Swan's lungs so heavily that each breath must be pushed out. Limpness lowered the arch in the mother's throat.

Down from the sky fell a soft tumult of snow. The flakes dissolved on the water; on the shores, the dam, and the brush they spread a cover. The downy mist thickened. An enemy could pounce from it. The swans heard the otters' cries but they could not see them. They could not see, in fact, to the other side of the pond. They heard also the brutal hoarseness of ravens, brawling over something, somewhere out there in the close white shower.

But loudest for the father may have been the calls of competing instincts. Surely he should be loyal first to his sick mate. He should stay here and protect her, helpless, needing him so desperately. His devotion to her was a lifelong emotion; his concern for the cygnets would pass before another brood could hatch.

Yet his full care of the young ones, recently, had strengthened his sense of responsibility for them. To save them, he should leave this vanishing marsh. He should take them to a new home, probably on the Red Rock Lakes, where he had spent his own years as a cygnet. Safety and food depended on water, and soon apparently none would be here.

To protect his mate or his fledglings — both calls rose from the deepest instincts in his nature. And the conflict may have been no less an anguish because conscious reasoning did not weigh it. Decided either way, one almost-irresistible urge must be denied.

He knew which call he would answer when he felt his wings lift. Into the dense enveloping snow he sped. He trumpeted to the cygnets and then slowed his flight, listening for the skitter of their feet, the air thrashed by their wings. When all three were aloft, a different note came into his voice. It spoke to his mate, though not with a summons. He was aware now that she could not rise. But he sent down his cry, for her to understand if she could. Twice he led the cygnets in low circles above the marsh, trumpeting to the white bird, so quiet upon the black pond. Finally her throat straightened, her bill lifted upward, and she trumpeted one answering call.

He turned his course west toward the Teton slope. Along the base of the mountains was a row of lakes, familiar enough so that he could find them in blind flying. He held his speed to the cygnets' and constantly urged them on, so that none would be lost. He was taking them to the smallest lake, on Mt. Moran, near the northern tip of the range. It could not be a home, for these lakes froze from shore to shore. But on its breadth were the tops of several muskrat lodges. One would be a roost where the family could await the end of the storm.

As they approached the lake, the snow thinned. Below was a gray and delicate lustre, circled by whitened thickets. The four swans coasted onto it. They glided first to the shallows for a meal of crowfoot. The silent unhurried fall began again. They climbed up on a lodge, and night crept in around them through the large wet flakes descending.

The father did not sleep. He could see but little — only a lightening in the smother where the water blurred into the shores. The ponderous mass of Mt. Moran he merely sensed. He slipped his bill under a wing in order not to feel the drop of the snow upon it.

He still was awake when the storm broke up. The mountain and the long range south took shape. The overhead thickness began to lift and shred. For a while clouds, luminous with moonlight, continued to cross the frosted blue of the dark night sky. Their shining passage seemed the only happening, now that the earth was covered by the wide monotony of the snow. As smoothly as swans the clouds appeared from over the Teton crest, to stream above the valley and beyond the eastern range. With a lingering hold one pulled away from another . . . lost the touch . . . moved on alone. Two united . . . blended . . . started to separate . . . clung . . . tore apart. Always they were changing, but their world did not change. It was a world of inviolate wildness.

A new wind swept the clouds away, and in the sky was only the moon, a hanging ball of light that dimmed the stars.

The bugling of an elk awakened the cygnets in the morning. He stood on a granite cliff above the lake and sent his challenge over the valley with a rising flow of notes almost as clear and vibrant as the Swan's.

The early light was coloring the snowy peaks with the nacreous pink of sea shells. Coming down the slope, the sunshine gilded the ivory crown upon the elk's head. It passed the pines and spruces at the shore and stretched back over the misty surface of the lake to the lodge.

The Swan allowed the cygnets to feed for a brief time. Soon he called them and rose from the pond to start their flight to the Red Rock Lakes. The sky felt crisp and electric, for with the storm's departure ozone from above the stratosphere was raining earthward. The pressure of the air was heightened, heightening in turn each animal's vitality. Never had the cygnets flown so swiftly.

Everything seemed changed, and for the better. That may have been the reason why the Swan reversed his course. Or possibly the danger to his mate was, after all, the stronger call. He circled back at the head of the valley, turning south instead of north. Setting an almost-adult speed for the young swans, he was following the Gros Ventre crest.

The indigo river shone between the white flats of the valley floor. One of its curves, there, held the marsh. The pond was smaller than before the tree fell, but it was not empty. The Swan was spiraling down.

His glide along the water stopped him near the dam. During the night the Beaver partly had repaired it, and the inflow of the brook had filled the marsh up to the level of the dam's unfinished top. The willow channels still were drained, but the surface spread back past the sedge beds, past the Swan's roost. Floating near the hillock was his mate.

He hastened toward the roost, so eagerly that now the ripples did not melt out from his sides but splashed away. The cygnets stopped at a bed of milfoil, which the lowering of the pond had brought within their reach.

The mother watched her family's return. Her eyes were more intense this morning, with a more accessible look. And there were other proofs that she was slightly stronger. Her wings lay higher on her back, and her throat was swinging slowly. Her head was turning in the sunlight. If she had swallowed more of the shot, she might not have recovered. She might not if the weather had remained depressing. But its most invigorating benefits had come together at her crisis. She would live, though never again to mother cygnets, for the poison had made her barren.

As the Swan approached, he thrust his head beneath the surface, tossed it back with a shower of crystal drops upon his wings. He beat the wings and half-rose from the water. Slowing the stroke, he let himself down but again reared, framed in his wings' great pulsing gleam of white.

The motion may have been stirred by instinct's memory of the autumn when they plighted their devotion. The ritual had been a kind of dance, in which the two, advancing toward each other, lifted from the water, breast to breast. This later day his mate could only once and briefly raise her wings — the merest opening along her sides, yet a wish expressed.

He tilted his bill as if to trumpet, but swung it down and glided closer to her. Both birds turned their attention to the sunny day, the cygnets, and the life that they would share once more, beginning with this new and silent clasping of their spirits.

The Beaver

THE BEAVER

✿

D own over the marsh spread the Swan's tender, desolate call. It seemed to speak of an end, perhaps the end of the old summer, leaving now, urging most of the birds to come south and the animals to find beds for their winter sleep. The tone sang in one's flesh:

Come. . . .

It was strong enough to reach every burrow and nest, and to enter the Beaver's house at the side of the pond. But the ears of the Beaver within were distracted by tappings upon his wall, by the knuckles of waves thudding upon the rubble of roots and sticks. The sounds were not right. His beaver instinct would not let him be comfortable while he was hearing them.

Each autumn since the house became his, when his father died, he had stuccoed the wall with mud. This fall he was not repairing it. The water had sucked last year's mud out of the wall, so that now when the ripples came slapping against the house, they would run into the pockets and knock on the resonant boughs.

The wind was dropping, however, as the afternoon passed;

the waves were quieting. Soon the Beaver could hear more of the happenings out of doors. At the top of his rounded roof was a hole, a flue, criss-crossed with sticks but not plastered. Sounds, as well as fresh air, entered it.

One that continued, regardless of wind, was the splash through the dam. The dam, like the house, was made of entangled sticks. The water did not go over it. Flowers and grass indeed grew on top; the water seeped through beneath them. The lively trickle, the spill, the curl down and break on the lower sticks, was a sheet of bright harmony that the Beaver knew as he knew his heartbeat. Let one timber wash out and open a larger pouring: at once he was aware of it. On this evening the sound was just as it should be.

Now too he heard more of the marsh voices. The dam had been built, by the Beaver's parents, across a small brook, where it entered Cottonwood Creek. The water that spread out then, in a many-fingered pond, had provided homes for uncounted creatures. Down the chinks in the Beaver's roof came the grunts and whinnies of courting moose, the cries of a raven, and the vehement quacks of ducks. Under the louder accents flowed the muted music of small birds, a chorus typical of September, when most of the arias were not full or complete, seeming no more than echoes of the hearty spring proclamations. A flock of mourning doves must be near the house. They were looping their cadences over it. Even the sound of the waves had not covered them, and when the water lay silent, the dove songs entered the house with a tolling clarity. A crash on the pond stopped them. The Osprey plunged down from a height for his evening fish, the spray fell on the doves, and their wings bore them away with vibrations so fine that they piped back a whistled tone.

In the Beaver's floor, at the top of his entrance tunnel, was a small pool, the water-door. It quivered as the hawk's dive shook the pond. The pool was still dimly luminous, although paler now than when sunshine fell on the pond outside, over the tunnel exit. Most of the light in the house came through the air hole. Above one chink the Beaver could see a leaf of the meadowsweet that grew on his thatch. Over it was a radiant sky. The Beaver's black and white vision did not tell him the sky had reddened. But he could watch it lose brightness. After the water-door was completely dark, the air hole still faintly showed. For a while a star pointed down through it.

No other beaver lived in this house. Only last March it was sheltering the Beaver's mate, three yearlings, and three two-year-olds. Trappers had caught the others. The Beaver had stayed alone, then, until recently, when a muskrat came in and appropriated one of the empty beds. She annoyed him, but he let her stay. Several weeks ago she had borne a litter of seven young. Now they and the mother were curled together, a steamy heap at the other end of the sleeping bench.

The floor of the house was on two levels. Beside the pool was a space where the Beaver would stop to eat and to dry off when he entered. The circular shelf for the beds was a little higher. The beds were covered with shredded wood and twigs, damp but well drained and clean. All through the summer the Beaver's family had seemed to be there, for the beds held their scent, each one so distinct that it almost was the creature himself. But finally the odors faded, and memory faded; and after the muskrat came, her alien scent, filling the house, had banished the little ghostly presences.

She was hungry now but was waiting for the too-slow thickening of night, in which one might escape a hunter by fleeing only a short way. Finally she drew herself out of the pile of her infants; with a melting dive, a flow of fur to the pool, she was gone. The Beaver continued to lie on his bed, while the star over him brightened and then swung past the latticed hole. He could hear the muskrats' small breathing and the moist lips of one, coaxing for a nipple. Very few animals could have been trusted so near undefended young. The Beaver was not tempted. He was an enemy of no creature, but he was irritated by these. With a hiss of distaste he rolled forward into the water-door, held his forepaws along his sides, and swung his tail diagonally to scull himself down through the tunnel.

The wall of the house flared wider beneath the pond, and the tunnel came out at its farthest point. The Beaver swam near the bottom until he had crossed to the opposite shore. No predator, watching for him, ever could guess where he would emerge. He came up tonight near the point of the water-meadow. At first he showed only his eyes, nose, and ears, which were all in one plane, letting him look, scent, and listen with no more than the flat triangular top of his head out of the water.

A single duck, black in the fading twilight, flew down the river, in over the water-meadow, across the pond, the dam, and the grove, out of sight. The Beaver started to paddle around, slowly, his nose pushing a wedge of silent ripples. He stroked with his webbed hind feet, left and right, stopped, idled along the water, swung his tail down to put himself under, and drifted back to the surface. He humped half out of it, loafing, as noiseless as the unruffled pond and the motionless trees below the faint glow hastening from the sky.

Tendrils of vapor were curling up from the water into the chill autumn air. They were signs, warnings of bare boughs, of snowbanks over the flowers, of ice shelving out from shore, of the dark winter inside his house. But the Beaver was warm tonight and dry in his dense fur, and was buoyant, relaxed as no creature can be on land, where muscles must always be tensed to support one's weight. He was not playing, but was feeling the sense of lightness that comes at nightfall.

When his family were here with him, they often had spent this time in a kind of unhurried game like hide-and-go-seek. One would slap his tail on the water and dive. Where would he rise? The others would circle about, watching. When one discovered a head breaking the surface, that fellow would splash and go under. Finally the parents would start to work, cutting the willows, aspens, and cottonwoods that furnished food and, after the bark was eaten, wood to strengthen the dam and house. The larger kits might continue to swim about for a while, perhaps with the younger kits on their backs. Then they would join their parents, and the smaller ones would amuse themselves with the silky mud. They loved heaping it into mounds, playing house, for building was one of their strongest urges. They would swim to the bottom, scoop a load of the mud up against their chests, push their way to shore, and plaster the new layer on, patting it with their deft little forepaws. Meanwhile they would murmur and squeal, in voices that human beings might not have distinguished from children's. They also liked to help cut the branches. Their older brothers and sisters would push them away, but their parents would let them try.

In the fall the aid of the smallest teeth had been welcome, for then the winter food supply must be cut quickly. The boughs were gnawed into sticks about beaver-length, dragged to the pond, and anchored down in the silt. After the pond froze over, a creature could swim out of his house, get a cutting, take it back in, and eat it without once showing himself. For that purpose the pond was created: so that water of greater than ice-depth would cover the house-door and the food. The Beaver never had hibernated, but he and his family would go inside for the winter and know almost complete safety. Even with snow on the house, air and a little light had entered, for the warm breaths from within had kept open the air hole. A wispy plume would curl up from the snow, often attracting coyotes, who would sniff it, tantalized. The beavers below would smell the scent of the enemy. But the coyotes, however hungry, always went on. They knew that there was no way they could break through the timbers and frozen mud.

That winter security was dependent on making preparations beforehand. But this year the Beaver was letting his house go to pieces, and so far he had not cut a single bough of his cold-weather food. For he was inclined to abandon the marsh. Maintaining it was a large task for one alone, and the motive was not there any longer. It had not been since the three nights last spring when he had found his family drowned, one after another, held on the pond floor by mechanisms of steel.

He could live somewhere else, join another beaver colony, have his own house, and be accepted by the resident clan as a kind of uncle, a beaver bachelor. He knew already where he might go — to the island in the Snake River, across from this marsh. When the dam went to pieces, as it soon would without upkeep, the marsh would be drained, and most of the water- and shore-loving plants would die. But he would not need them. In the island grove was enough food to support at least one beaver besides the colony already there. He was spending most of his nights on the island, and it was beginning to feel like home.

The wedge of ripples steadied and pointed east, faster now, along one of the bays in the willow thickets. At the end the Beaver slipped out of the water quietly. He shook himself, listened, tested the air; then started on to the river.

He walked on the soles of his pigeon-toed hind feet and on the tips of his forefeet, yet his long hind legs lifted his back high above his shoulders. With his nose toward the ground he swayed ahead at his best pace, an irregular trot. Out of the water he could escape no nimble-footed enemy. He was not even a fast fighter; he could only hook his chisel-teeth into a predator's flesh and hold on. Therefore he was hurrying. It was his prudent way to avoid emergencies, not to rely on brilliance in meeting them. The same kind of foresight had impelled him to build dams and houses, and to store food. It stirred in him now. His ambition would strengthen each night when he left the marsh and the loneliness here that was paralyzing his provident urges.

At the riverbank he turned upstream to compensate for the pull of the current, but finally plunged in, and, driving with feet and tail, crossed to the island. He came out in a small cove.

On one side of it was the rubble house of the island clan. The eldest male of this family was approaching, towing a cottonwood pole down his dry canal. The two met soon after the Beaver climbed up on the shore. No sign passed between them. A baldly direct encounter would have embarrassed them, but they read each other's intentions. From the quiet, practical way that the Beaver would arrive, cut his food, eat it, groom his fur, rest, and depart, the resident felt that this stranger would not be lazy. He would not steal from the clan's winter stores. The elder's ignoring of him told the Beaver that he was acceptable.

The Beaver let himself down the side of the empty canal and started along to the northern shore. The upper end of the ditch was there. Except now when the river was low, its water entered the ditch and poured down the island. The owners had curved the canal through stands of aspens, in order to float their wood to their door.

Perhaps the Beaver would choose the mouth of the ditch as his new homesite. The river was deep; he could not build a house in it, but it never would freeze. He could dig into the bank, from below the top of the water, and burrow a rising tunnel with a dry room at the end. The room would be near the surface. He would break the earth over it for an air hole, and pile a small mound of sticks above, to keep the snow loose.

From a home like that he could come out to forage all winter. Nevertheless he should have a stockpile of cuttings under the water, from which he could draw on the coldest days. It seemed likely that he could anchor it to a snag he had discovered, one caught in the river-bed.

Such living arrangements were different from those of his past, and different from any others that he had seen. Yet he was able to work them out, because he had an adaptability rare in wild animals. He did not have in his head very much of the brain tissue which gives human beings the power to reason. But perhaps he used what he had with exceptional willingness — with the same exertion that he put into his physical efforts.

As he walked along in the canal, he could hear ahead a scratching of leafy twigs. He paused, sniffed, and recognized the scent of one of the young island beavers. The shadows were hiding her, but he knew from seeing her on bright moon-lit nights that she was a two-year-old, darker-furred than the older beavers, smoother, rounder, and with a little blunt nose. Now she was coming forward, dragging a branch. He climbed out of the ditch, to make way, but placed a bit of his castor scent in her path. It was a message for her alone; he had left none when he met her father. The two passed with no other communication.

He went into the ditch again. The overhead leaves did not open for even the small ray of a star, but the ditch led him on to the paler night over the river. Back from the shore stood a huddle of frail white aspen trunks. He would gnaw down one tree, eat some of the bark, and see whether the tree could be fixed on the sunken snag.

He moved in the careful way of a creature who always is listening, but he set to work without stopping to reconnoiter. Far away on the sagebrush plain a coyote was baying. A coyote or human being, both enemies, could cross over the river. But few of them would. An otter might; yet the Beaver felt a new sense of security here, for the island was much less accessible than the marsh.

He rose on his hind feet, close to an aspen trunk. Turning his head across it, he sank his teeth in the bark. The upper two chisels gripped in, and he drove the lower pair toward them with a push that came all the way from his flat naked tail, braced behind him.

The teeth did not penetrate very far; they were dull from their lack of use. His forepaws were on the trunk, one above, one below his mouth. They clutched on the bark as he drew back his teeth, drove them in with a harder bite, out and in, each time farther. Holding them there, he twisted his head, prying, pulling the chip. It came loose and he dropped it.

But he must sharpen his teeth. These claw-shaped orange chisels had hard enamel fronts; on the inner sides were much softer. By rasping the ends together, he gave them a finer edge. The next chip was cut faster, and his teeth became keener with every bite. They would be more comfortable if he should start to gnaw regularly. They never stopped growing and were nearly as long now as the claws of a bear.

He kept moving around the tree, whittling into his notch from all sides. He heard a split in the wood. Ready to run, tense, he waited. The tree continued to stand; so he bit out several more, shallower chips. With a faint shriek, then, the core of the aspen broke. The tree came down toward him, on him, but only its limber top branches struck him, and he was not hurt.

The juice in the bark had tempted his appetite. He curled his forepaws around a bough, bit it off clean as a fractured icicle, and sat up with the branch crosswise in his mouth, turning it out and down, while his chisels peeled off the bark. He soon had finished that branch and another, and was ready to take the tree into the river.

The moon was up now, but its light never penetrated far into the water. As on all nights, he must work chiefly by intuition and touch. The snag he had found was off the tip of the island, where the current divided and was not very swift. Taking the stub of the tree in his mouth, he slipped into the river and dived. The green wood sank easily. He could remain underwater for a time that human beings measure as five minutes; so he waited to fix the aspen carefully in a crotch in the snag.

After he rose, he circled above it, watching the surface for signs of its drifting up. But it stayed. Other boughs could be fastened under and into it, and the heap could be weighted with stones. It would be a food supply close to his door.

As he returned to the shore, he swam to the spot where he would start digging his tunnel. Swinging under the top of the water, he clawed out a few pawfuls of earth from the bank. The number of rocks in it were a difficulty, but they probably would not make the tunnel impractical. A very strenuous time lay ahead, to get his tunnel dug before the ground froze, and his wood all cut. But after the new home was established, he could live with more ease than he ever had known, with no dam to be kept in repair, and a house that never would need to be plastered.

It seemed decided, then, that he would move to the island. He was contented, almost happy, as he sat on the bank, looking out over the river, while he combed his fur with the double, fine-toothed nails that he had on two toes of his hind feet. He had not gone far with the grooming, however, when some strand in the wind caught his attention. He paused; then turned to face toward the trees. Somewhere back in the shadows his new young friend must be watching.

The Beaver went back to the marsh to sleep. Most of the animals were at home now. The night prowlers had returned to their shelters, and the daytime creatures were not yet astir. The marsh seemed deserted, but actually no place else in the valley, unless another marsh, was so richly alive.

As the Beaver came in from the river bank, he saw the Varying Hare, crouched under the brush. She needed that sort of home, one she could enter or leave in haste. In the boughs close above her perched the small birds who feel lonely in tall trees, birds of the air but also of earth: bluebirds, chickadees, juncos, and yellow warblers. The ducks floated in the bays, or, like the Merganser, had nestled into the reed-grass. The Trumpeter Swan and his family, wanting isolation, were finding it on an island of sedges. The plants were sheltering many insects, too. A thistle had given a refuge to the Mosquito.

The water itself was a home. The Leopard Frog had spent some of the night in his puddle. Now he had backed himself under a stone, but he slowly closed one eye, later the other, to freshen the view of his own miniature marsh. The Leech snuggled roundly against a water-lily stem. The Snail had glued himself to it. The Scud was clutching the edge of a floating aspen leaf with most of his thirty feet. Drifting about in the water, with no more substantial home, were the tiny animals of the plankton.

The small tubes of mud and leaf scraps on the bottom were shelters, not merely found but built, by bloodworms and caddisworms. None was empty. If one ever was vacated, bell-animals moved in, surely with satisfaction. Even the burrowers had their preferences — bristleworms for the softness of ooze, clams for the firm sand — and had found homes as they liked them.

The Osprey had his perch in the dead cottonwood tree that helped to support the dam, and the wall of the Beaver's own house was a haven for a Trout, a garter snake, and a water shrew. These creatures and most of the others could sense that the winter soon would destroy or close many nooks. But the marsh would have substitutes, and the plants would grow again by the time they were needed — if the dam were still here. All these favorite crannies had been supplied by the dam.

It had trapped the brook's load of soil, that might have been lost in the river. It had formed the pond, furnishing moisture for the seeds that had fallen here. Even in dry years the marsh was green and luxuriant.

Only the Beaver may have conceived of the pond's ever vanishing. But the animals did know that winter brought changes, and that many must move. Had the prospect, that night, intensified the home-loving emotion of the small beasts sheltered in such immense numbers throughout the marsh?

The Beaver cut a withe for himself as he left the willow thickets. He towed it to the bank at the side of his house and climbed out to eat it before going to sleep. The moon was sinking into the tall cottonwood trees behind him, but its last light was tracing in silver the familiar boundaries of the marsh. One side of the pond was marked by a flowing gleam, where the water swung up to his dam. On the opposite shore, his willows merged in a fine feathery-leaved mist. The backwash was only a mysterious blending of dull and shining shadows, but outside of it was a wide silver glitter, the brook splashing into the pond over the stones it had dropped at the end of its little journey.

As the brook drained through the pond to the dam, it was merely the movement of water through water, a drawing-forward like the submerged wake behind fish. That idling current had given the Beaver much pleasure. He would miss the relaxed sense of it when the tumultuous river, instead, flung itself past his door.

The whole marsh was his home, and was at least as dear to him as the separate shelters were to the other animals. But the skeleton of his grief stood over it, like the dead tree, prop in the dam, whose gaunt arms the moon now was whitening.

That night was exactly as long as the day to come, for the sun, swinging south for the winter, had reached the equator. In many parts of the world this was a time of disturbed weather. Jackson Hole lay in the path of one storm, a polar front crossing Idaho toward the Teton range.

The winds and the falling air pressure had added their teasing to the animals' urgent sense of the coming winter. The Beaver within his house was unable to sleep. He washed his fur, smoothed it with the claws of his forefeet; next went over it with his two combing claws. He closed his eyes, but soon opened them and repeated the grooming.

He had a reason for uneasiness that most of the animals did not know. Late in the night he had seen an Otter arrive. Twice on his summer travels the Beaver had met with otters, but never before at the marsh. While he was sitting beside the house, peeling his willow withe, the dark sinuous creature had risen over the dam. The Beaver froze, as his intuition gathered all its misgivings about otters. An oblique look passed between the two. The Beaver, with sturdy daring, challenged first. He dived, smacking his tail on the pond with a slap that meant what a slap does to every animal. Then he had entered his house, even more angry than frightened. But he could not sleep. All his senses were waiting for the enemy to emerge through the water-door.

Thus had this day begun. About noon the Beaver heard the creak of wood splitting. Could another beaver be felling a tree? A tree surely was coming down. The snap of boughs breaking, and a violent splash on the pond, sent him hurrying out.

A tree did lie in the pond, but the wind had overturned it. The trunk was under the surface, and half the boughs. Others, cracked off, were drifting away. Drifting, and too fast! Their speed and the pounding new roar opened his mind to a shock. The tree was the one which had braced his masonry. Its fall wrecked the dam to which his family had given incessant minute care, night and day, for two generations. Short of a life and death struggle, there was no greater emergency.

The possibility of a life and death struggle did loom. For the Otter was here, seemingly everywhere as he climbed on the rubble, sculled in the pond, and waded its borders. The Beaver went back in his house.

Through all the afternoon he was there, watching his waterdoor drain away . . . soon below the firm rim in the floor, now exposing the matted-root walls of the tunnel, now so far down the incline that when he went to his exit he must walk, rather than swim.

He kept going, to peer out at the devastation. Some of the fish had escaped, but stranded pools had trapped more and had trapped other small, uncomprehending creatures, who had died with no outcry. A moose calf, trying to cross the exposed silt, had drowned in it. A second otter had come, and another hunter, a Mink. Finally, as if to cover the unhappy scene, the sky had released a deluge of snow.

The Beaver could not understand the related logic in these events, how the disastrous wind and the arrival of wandering predators all were a part of the turn into winter. Only one thing was clear — that, as soon as he could, he must start to rebuild the dam.

A rational kind of thinking would have suggested that this was the time to desert the marsh. The fall of the tree simply had hastened the loss of the pond. It would drain anyway, soon after he moved to the island. The snow was a warning that he should be digging his new burrow there. Why wait; he had nothing to take, nothing to be made ready except his own urge to go.

For six years the slightest change in the dam's liquid murmur had started him cutting sticks and scooping up mud. The chain of action had become automatic — and irresistible. He could have left when the sounds in the dam assured him that it was solid. From this ominous pouring nothing could draw him away.

He crouched in his exit, half-sick with impatience. Finally one otter left, and the other crawled into a hollow log in the grove. Night came, its darkness made even more dense by the falling snow. It was a cover in which he could work with few pauses for caution.

He would fill the hole with an aspen and weave willow boughs into it. He would weight down the brush with stones and cement it with mud. Additions on top would raise it.

If the aspen were not to be carried away by the flow, it should be wider, but not much, than the gap. He knew exactly the tree, one on the bank near his house. As is often the habit of beavers, he had left that accessible tree uncut. And now had come the emergency that his intuition may have foreseen.

He always entered the grove through the stub of a ditch that he had started to build, once, mistakenly, in the too-high bank. Now he climbed up out of the end, beside his tree — but stopped. Under the aspen stood a Moose, a newcomer, larger than any bull he had seen. Moose were usually no more than a vague threat, but something in the too-quiet tension of this bull restrained the Beaver. He would hesitate to work there below him. He sniffed, listened, started to back down into the ditch. He climbed up again . . . but could not bring himself to go out. For the present, at least, he could not have that tree.

He almost did return for it; the tree he cut back in the water-meadow took so long a time to drag across the drying floor of the pond. But finally he reached the dam with it and found it broad enough to catch on the sides of the hole.

Next he began his trips to the willow thickets. The slim withes, severed easily, were ideal for the filling. He could bring back two at once, sometimes three, but many were needed. The snow ceased about midnight, and the moon came out; the night wore on. He would work the willow branches into the aspen with his forepaws, placing them parallel with the flow. Across it they might have stopped the drainage faster but would have made a weaker foundation. The Beaver was not patching the dam for one night. His repairs would be fully as strong as the building done by his parents.

He dug his stones from the bank. When he could lift them, he carried them against his chest, walking upright. Some he rolled with his forepaws or, when they were too heavy, pushed with his side and hip. He piled the rocks on the dike and over-laid them with mud from the floor of the pond. If he had been starting a new dam, he would have let the normal flow fill in the small chinks with its debris of silt, leaves, twigs, and insects' bodies. Mud gave a quicker plastering. Containing roots of water-plants, it made the masonry tight.

The new section was holding back just a little more of the water than the brook was bringing into the marsh. The tide had turned. The edge of the pond had started to rise on the slanting floor.

The Beaver did not stop work to look pridefully at his accomplishment. It was the mate of the Trumpeter Swan whose heart eased with relief. She had floated all night on the shrinking pond. She had felt the surface settling beneath her, had felt the marsh, her world — in fact her life — sinking away. But now she could sense the lessening of the current's pull on her legs. She could see the water begin to creep up the silt. Receiving the boon with a swan's poise, she laid her head back between her wings and slept.

The night would end soon and the Beaver would have to go into his house. But first he would cut a new aspen and more willow stems for the next layer in the dam. It would save time if he could use the aspen upon the bank. From the scent of the Moose, he knew that the huge beast still stood near the tree. Should he not risk approaching him?

He started to gnaw the trunk on the side away from the bull, but he did not feel safe. He walked back in the grove, once more gnawed at his tree, went down in the pond, and returned. Finally the aspen fell, with its top hanging over the shore. He cut off the trunk. Now he was ready to pull the branches along to the dam.

The Moose had climbed down off the bank. He stood in the shallow water, eating at the aspen leaves. The Beaver, intent on his purpose, did not sense that he was pulling the Moose's food away from him. He fixed his teeth in the bark, started forward, felt a drag, and pulled more strongly.

The bull reared, a black tower of rage, hurled his monstrous weight down toward the Beaver, and struck with the points of his hoofs. The blow would have gone through flesh as through muck, but the Beaver had dodged. The water was deep enough now to allow him to swing in it. Legs and tail stroked convulsively, and he sculled toward his tunnel.

The hoofs were again in the air, were lunging down, crashed through the water. But the Beaver had reached his entrance and was swimming wildly up into his house.

He still was not safe. The Moose was stomping the roof. At the first blow, a rain of earth fell from the rubble. At the second, a shattered timber came through, killing one of the muskrats. The earthen plastering drained in sheets from the loosened boughs; the whole house seemed collapsing. With his antlers the Moose was raking off sticks from the top. Now he was stomping again; a hoof came down into the air hole. It would have crushed any creature directly beneath it, but the Beaver and the surviving muskrats cowered under the low-angled wall. They were trying blindly to shrink away from the horror, in this total dark, thick with the scent released by their terror.

Unable to break through the roof, the Moose tried to demolish the wall at the water's edge, where it widened. His blows crushed the entrance tunnel, locking the creatures within. But the pitiful heap of trash continued to hold an arch over their heads.

For an instant, silence; then the sound of flung gravel told that the bull had lunged up the bank. His hoofs pounded upon the floor of the grove, a beat quickly diminishing. He had given up trying to reach the Beaver and was racing away from the marsh.

For a long time the Beaver sat motionless. But finally his steady spirit turned back to life. He licked the palms of his forepaws and rubbed them over his cheeks, starting to clean the dirt out of his fur.

With teeth like the Beaver's a creature could gnaw his way out of a house, as well as cut timbers to build it. He chiseled off some of the broken boughs and pulled others aside with his forepaws. When he began, the birds were just breaking the night with the points of their chirps. By the time he sculled out of his hole, the sun was rising over the glistening eastern peaks.

The water had flowed back past the sedge beds, almost to the willow bays, and the pond was deep enough for him to swim under the top. He went at once to the dam. The part he had fixed held secure and firm. It would have to be twice as high, but perhaps he should not finish it for a few more days. A lower drainage, just now, would take away the bodies of yesterday's victims, a need that the Beaver could sense this morning.

He turned away from the dam and, swimming slowly, looked over the marsh. The flat valley floor was white, and the mountains were crisply frosted. Many creatures were out and moving as if they enjoyed the novelty of the snow-covered world. On the unbroken side of the dam was a hole with tiny tracks leading to it. A red-backed mouse had decided on this place to make a snow burrow. He had gone in and could not have come out yet, for a spider web closed his entrance. Near it a chickadee had alighted to dust in the crystals. Beside the small oval cup he had hollowed, were the patterns of angel wings, beaten down as he flew away.

The Beaver's house was an ugly black-trampled wreck in the clean marsh. Now, even in daylight, he would fill at least one of the breaks. Getting a few twigs from above the bank, he thrust them into the hole. From the pond floor he brought earth, staggering up the sloping wall of the house on his hind feet. He plastered the mud into the hole, laid a few twigs across it, and trampled them into the mud.

He had not seen the house built; he had not helped to pile timbers up to the floor above water-level, and then weave the walls to their tapering peak. He had not made the original tunnel, so strong, so smoothly lined with roots, and yet with the accidental look of a thing done by a wild animal. The house had come to him finished. Should he be inclined to rebuild it, his innate skill must direct him.

He would leave the demolished house before he would the dam; but perhaps he would leave neither. He felt possessive about the house. He was not happy to see it a shambles. If he repaired it and then completed the dam, the season might be too late to start digging the burrow. It might be that he could not move to the island this autumn, but his house and his marsh would be snug.

Going away, abandoning all the destruction, would have been easier. But instinct is not so simple in its objectives. More often than intellect, possibly, it requires the hard choice. The command is to wait and to grope, to labor, to risk life, as frequently as it is to indulge oneself; and not only for the Beaver. The other animals, too, followed instinctive discipline to the good ways that work permanently. That is what wildness is — to follow the inner impulse without wilfulness, and sensitively.

The morning was cold and fresh, for the air currents after the storm were bringing down ozone. The air smelled as if it were sky that one breathed, as indeed it was. But there was another, even more stimulating scent.

The Beaver paddled along the surface, letting the odor draw him forward. It guided him to the mouth of the brook.

Crouched there under the trees was another beaver, his young friend from the river colony. This was the first time she had left her family to go away from the island alone. It was a daring thing to be at a strange marsh, and in the daytime. She felt shy and lost, and had pulled herself deep in the covering of her glossy dark fur. She should be under some roof, not out in a world so revealing, with snow everywhere, and above her the fragile brilliance of the sunlight among the white aspen trunks.